ENVY

THE DARK KINGS

CONTENT WARNINGS

Content Warnings: The Dark Kings is a high steam, high action dark romance series. The following content warnings should be considered before reading them: Dealing with previous trauma, assault, miscarriage, murder, sex trafficking, drug use, depression, anxiety, PTSD, bipolar disorder, gun violence, kidnapping, sexism, prostitution, elements of BDSM such as impact play and restraints, electro stimulation, knife play, primal play, CGL relationship, Shabari, profanity and sexually explicit scenes. This is a Why Choose romance. If you have any questions please reach out to the author directly at info @nikkirome.com.

To all the smut lovers, may Nico's insanity bring you peace at night. If it's not peace he provides you then relish in his chaos. May this book make you wet even on the driest of days.

Envy by Nikki Rome

Published by Rome Publishing Group

www.NikkiRome.com

For permissions contact:

Info@NikkiRome.com

Cover by Alt19 Creative

CONTENTS

CHAPTER ONE

NICO

I never understood why people use one word to describe rage. It is an insane emotion, yet the word that is used to express the worst kind of anger doesn't do the feeling any justice. For me, rage is more than just an emotional response. My body physically feels sick. The tension that runs through me makes me feel as if my muscles will snap and my heart will explode. It is unbearable. On the outside, I look like a monster. Or at least that's what people tell me. The years of shrinks with different diagnoses never helped. Medications turned me into a zombie and therapists are all fucking assholes. Yup, that about sums it up. Where some people get depressed and hide under the covers, others get sad and feel better if they cry. I'm a person who can never subdue the beast. Anger is a relief in relation to rage. It's always there, like a comforting blanket. Well, that was until Valentina.

Someone stole the only good thing I had in my life and it was entirely my fault. Guilt once again ate away at me every single day. There wasn't a moment that went by that I didn't hate myself for what had happened, but that same guilt just spiked more anger within me. I was vibrating with it, and even those close to me wouldn't get near me. My brothers by choice, Dante and Ares, were at a loss, and I couldn't blame them. They should hate me as much as I hate myself. It's been two weeks since the dreaded night they took her and as each day passed it got worse, not better. I rolled over in the mud and grass by the lake. Our property was surrounded by woods, and this quiet area behind the house had become my domain over the years. My body hurt all over as I stretched, which wasn't surprising. I hadn't spent more than a handful of nights in the main house. It was too painful. Even though she was only with us for a few weeks, I saw her everywhere I turned. So instead, I found solace in the darkness of the overgrown landscaping. The weather was cooling, so I'd sleep during the day under the thick foliage and stayed awake at night. Movement kept me warm, and I'd run or hunt. I deserved to suffer alone. Everything I touched turned to shit, anyway.

Every once in a while, Ares would bring me someone that he and Dante believed had information about where she was. They were all dead ends, though. Literally dead ends. As in, they never left alive. In the past, killing the awful people of the world would bring me calm, but for the last two weeks, it has just enraged me more. They didn't stop looking though: we would never stop looking. Which is why when I heard Ares' thick boots making their way toward me through the brush, I had just assumed it would be another person for me to question, another person for me to kill.

"Get up."

"Fuck off."

"Get up, Nico. Don't make me ask you again."

I held my hands over my eyes, trying to block out the morning sun. "Leave me alone."

"If you don't get the fuck up and head to the house, I will drag your ass there myself."

Ares wasn't a small man by any means. We were equal in height, but I had more muscle mass, which made me a great deal heavier. In a normal situation, his idle threats wouldn't mean much, but I was still fucked up from the night before and it would be stupid for me to think I was in any condition to fight him off.

"I'm not going to the house."

"Yeah, you are. You need to get cleaned up. We are leaving today."

"Leaving for where?"

"Sicily. I found Valentina."

He turned on his heels and headed back toward the house. He found Valentina. I sat up, my heart racing in both fear and excitement. Ares wouldn't lie about something like this.

"How?" I shouted after his retreating form.

"I found Alessia. Clean yourself up and we'll talk."

Alessia, the bitch who started all of this. The woman in black, the one who ruined my life not once, but twice. Seeing her that night was like seeing a ghost. I had convinced myself the lies they told about her were true. That she was dead, gone, never to come after me again. But that wasn't true, none of it was true, and as if no time had passed, she waltzed back into my life and destroyed me again. I pushed myself up to my feet. If Ares was right and Valentina was in Sicily, then I was in for a world of shit. I hadn't been back there since everything happened and now I had no choice. I wouldn't let them go without me, not if there was a chance to get my beautiful girl back.

An hour later, I was showered and dressed. I looked in the mirror and barely recognized myself. Love was something Dante never believed in, but ever since I was a kid, I could see how healing and perfect true love could be. It was a constant argument between us as we grew up and likely led to the reasoning behind our relationship now. Valentina had been promised to him at a young age and although he wanted her, he never believed he could love her the way she deserved. Most of the men in his family treated women like commodities. Nothing more than a hot pussy to fuck and a pretty accessory for others to envy. I always assumed his insistence that true love didn't exist was because of that, but I could never reconcile his grandparents' relationship. I had no one growing up and when I was the snot-nosed kid who was getting his ass beat by Dante's cousin Luca, he protected me and took me in. It wasn't long after that we all became best friends. I basically lived with Dante for the rest of my childhood, which meant I saw first-hand what true love was. His grandparents had it and I hung on every word his grandfather said to his grandmother. I committed it to memory because even then, in my scrambled kid mind, I knew there was something better in this life.

"Welcome back to the land of the living." Dante said as I walked into the office.

"Yeah, thanks."

"We leave in two hours. Ares was up all night again and we've been going about this all wrong."

"What do you mean?"

"We had assumed, since Matteo Costa took her that night, that he still had her."

"Doesn't he?"

"No."

"Then where is she?"

"With Alessia. We believe she's been there the whole time."

The impact of that statement was not lost on me. Alessia De Bartoli was a vicious bitch who ran one of the largest families in Sicily.

"How did they get her to work with them? The Costas are nothing compared to Alessia."

"That, my brother, is something you will have to ask her when you see her."

"When will I see her?"

"Ares set up a meeting, and she agreed only if she could speak with you."

I fell back into the chair in front of his desk. She didn't get to control me. Not anymore. Yet here we were at her mercy because she had the only thing of importance that we had in this world.

"You know you can't kill her."

"Why the fuck not?"

"Don't be a fool, Nico. Alessia De Bartoli has risen to the top in a very short time. Ares and I know her brother is nothing but a figurehead. She is the one who calls the shots. But you knew that already, didn't you?"

I looked away from him, refusing to keep eye contact while he questioned me again over my decisions.

"I just want to know why, Nico. You still haven't told us why you lied to us."

"It wasn't a lie, and none of it matters anymore."

"Yes, it does. You endangered Valentina, and I won't stand for that."

"My past had nothing to do with her getting kidnapped," I insisted, even though that wasn't true either, "The Costas would have come for her, anyway. You know that."

"The Costas we can handle. The largest crime family in all of Sicily is a different story. We are going to her, which means we will abide by the rules set forth. We will get Valentina and we will bring her home. If you fuck any of this up by killing someone you shouldn't, you will open us to a massive risk. Valentina is more important than you popping off at someone like a fucking child."

Dante's anger was palpable. I could feel it rising with mine and it never did. He was the one who always kept a cool head, or at least hid his feelings. He was right, and I hated it. Once we had her back, I'd go back to deal with Alessia. I should have done it the day she showed up at the club. Going after her now would be the last thing I ever did. I won't let her live, but I'm not an idiot. Her brother will have me killed just for thinking about it.

"Come on, Ares is waiting for us to eat."

"I'm not hungry."

"I don't care. You will eat and drink fucking water and you will only take the drugs I give you. You are out of control, Nico, and if I could leave you behind and do this, then I would. But she wants you, not me, not Ares, you. Which means you need to pull your fucking shit together and follow orders for once in your life. Meet me in the kitchen."

Dante pushed back from his desk and left. I hated him at that moment, but it was only because he was right. The downside of my manic episodes was the worthless feeling that never went away. I drowned those feelings in drugs, liquor and fights, which left me beaten down and useless. That's where I was right now, a useless piece of shit that my best friend would have left if he could. That fucking hurt more than anything else.

I went to my desk and pulled out my phone. The night they took Valentina, I put it in there. I turned it on to find a ton of messages and began filtering through them as I headed to the kitchen.

"Hey, you okay?" Ares asked when I sat at the table.

"Yeah, I'm fine."

I reached for a cup of coffee and took a sip. Coming back to the land of the living was never easy. After two weeks of internal chaos, something as simple as a cup of coffee felt strange in my hand. I reached for the serving dishes and made myself a plate. I had no idea how much I could eat, but Dante was watching me like a hawk and I wasn't in the mood for anymore of his shit.

"Heads up," he said and threw a bottle of pills in my direction.

"Take two of those now." I looked down to find my name on the label. Nothing like a couple of Xanax to calm the nerves, I thought as I opened it and did as he asked.

At least he wasn't making me deal with this whole thing sober.

"We should try to head out soon. I told them we'd fly out at ten."

"That's fine. We will leave after Nico eats."

"I called our staff at the villa. Since it's been so long, I wanted to let them know we were coming. They will have everything we need to stay."

"Stay? Why are we staying? I thought Dante said we were bringing her home."

"We are. But we don't know what Alessia wants in return, so we don't know how long that will take," Dante said.

"Besides, her home is with us, not this house. She needs to learn that it doesn't matter where we are. As long as we are together, she is home."

Ares and his bleeding heart were enough to annoy me on a good day. Today, it just pissed me off. I hated everything about Sicily. It was filled with nothing but terrible memories and I tied almost every one of those memories to the Da Bartolis.

CHAPTER TWO

VALENTINA

"They are coming for you tonight," Alessia said as she stood behind me, brushing my hair, "We will need to get you ready for them."

My heart skipped a beat at her comment. The last two weeks had been a range of unhealthy emotions and now I was questioning if Alessia was the terrible woman who helped the Costas or just someone who was thoroughly misunderstood. She had told me from the beginning that I would be safe and that Dante, Ares and Nico would come for me, but she never told me when and she never told me how.

"Do you love them?" she asked as she stared at my reflection in the mirror.

"I do. More than anything."

"Love is such a fickle thing. It doesn't matter if it's love between two people who choose to love one another or if it's love between a parent and a child. It's not everlasting, like people think. But you know that already, don't you?"

I nodded. Alessia seemed to know things about me she shouldn't. For someone I had never met in my life, she knew about my father, my upbringing, she knew about the guys and even the arrangement with the Costas. I didn't understand what she gained by taking me here, and I still don't. In the short time we'd been together, I'd learned that her brother runs a crime family here in Sicily and yet I still don't know what her role is with everything. She's been by my side since the night we arrived and has become a friend in an otherwise miserable situation. When I looked up that night and saw Matteo Costa looking down at me, I had believed my life was over. However, when I woke up on a private plane with my head in Alessia's lap while she ran her hands through my hair, I learned things changed quickly in this world.

"I want to get you ready for them. I have an entire crew of people coming to pamper us. We will be washed, waxed, glossed, and dressed to the nines! It will be so much fun."

"Alessia, you don't have to go out of your way for me. I'm thankful enough that you protected me from the Costas, but I'm sure the guys won't mind if I look just as I am right now."

"You are so young and naïve, my dear girl. Men like the Corsettis don't like plain Jane. They might pretend to now, but could you imagine the judgement from the other wives in your city if you don't maintain appearances? They are judgmental bitches. Even the wives here."

"Is that why you don't have many friends?"

"I don't have any friends. My brother is all I have in this world, and that's fine. He underestimates me, but I think he's learning what I'm capable of now that we are older. Women are catty and evil, except you. I know you think your father did terrible things to you, but by keeping you locked away as he did, he kept you from the influence of others. It's that influence that turns humans into terrible people."

I watched as she flitted around my room, pulling clothes from my closet and laying them out on the bed. "Here, put this on so you are comfortable. Everyone should be here soon, and they will get started on our makeovers when they arrive."

Makeovers seemed a bit much, but I wasn't in a position not to follow directions. Alessia was kind, but I was still a stranger in her home. I was grateful she kept me from the Costas, but bringing me to Italy rather than bringing me back to the guys didn't make much sense. I had asked why, but all she would say was, wait and see. Today I would learn what her ulterior motive has been all along because I suspected she wasn't befriending me out of the goodness of her own heart.

By the time Alessia's team of people thoroughly primped us, it was nearly dinner. I had experienced nothing like I had today. There wasn't a hair left on my body except for my head and eyebrows. They painted my nails a bright shade of red that matched my toes, and my make-up resembled something out of a movie. I stood in the mirror of my bathroom and took in my appearance. I had put some weight on, which was a good thing. The food here was amazing, and I was gaining my strength back from the time my father had had me locked away. Between the time I spent with Dante, Ares and Nico and my time here in Sicily, I was feeling stronger than I had in a long time. Alessia had chosen a white wrap dress for me to wear. It was silk and felt amazing over my skin. The heels I had on were worth more than my life and I was terrified I'd do something ridiculous and break a heel. What I had thought were just rhinestones ended up being diamonds that ranged in size. The woman looking back at me looked happy, healthy and ready to move forward in this world, and the ache in my chest was finally letting up in anticipation of seeing my men again.

The situation could have been way worse, but missing them was a pain I had never experienced before. I'd never loved someone enough to miss them. There were days I had been here, and I thought I could never push through the pain. Dante, Ares and Nico promised I would never be without one of them, but here I was alone in a strange home with a strange family, and they were nowhere in sight.

"Sei così bella, I can see why they want to keep you." Alessia's voice brought me from my thoughts.

"Thank you."

"Are you sure you want them? I can provide you with a wonderful life in Sicily. I've seen how much you like it here. It could be like this forever."

I reached for her hand and held it in mine. "Alessia, thank you for such a generous offer, but we both know my place is with them. I was promised to Dante as a young girl and I have always set my heart on him."

"And the others?"

I smiled. "They are like the bonus scenes in a fantastic book or movie. My love for them isn't any less than my love for Dante. They are my future."

"Just because men told you what your future would be doesn't mean it has to be true."

"I know. But this is the life I am choosing for myself. Besides, I have taken up so much of your time while I've been here. I'm sure you want to get back to your normal life."

"Things won't always be as you hope, Bellezza. Everything is about to change again for you, and if you decide it's not what you want, you can always come back to me."

I didn't know what she meant by that, but it wasn't time to dig into it all. Dante, Ares and Nico would be here tonight, and I was desperate to see them. "Are you ready?"

"Yes. Will they be here soon?"

"They are already here."

I embraced her, my excitement overwhelming me. I stayed close as we walked through the main part of the house. They hadn't allowed me to move around it freely, but Alessia took me just about everywhere. When we got to the courtyard, I took in a deep breath of the ocean air. I would miss it when we left for New York.

"Come, I want you to wait out here while I meet with them. Then you will make your grand entrance and take their breath away!"

I sat at the small bistro table she had pointed to and watched her head back inside. A guard came out and stood watch and then her brother made his way into the courtyard and walked towards me.

"Well, aren't you just a pretty little thing?" he said as he leaned in and placed a kiss on my cheek. Massimo De Bartoli creeped me out. There was no better way to explain it. The way he watched my every move made me nervous he was going to pounce. The first night we were here, I heard Alessia arguing with him in the hallway. She had forbidden him from coming in and bothering me, and for some insane reason he listened to her.

"Hello, Massimo. Good to see you."

"Are you sure? You've been at my home for a week now and you still haven't come to visit with me."

"Alessia keeps me quite busy."

"I'm sure she does," he laughed a shallow laugh and then continued, "So today is the day you think you will leave?"

"Yes, I will go home with Dante, Ares and Nico as planned."

"That's what she told you?"

"Yes. Why do you ask?"

"My sister is... how do you say?? Difficult... no, no, manipulative."

"Is there something I should know?"

He took a seat across from me at the table. "All I am saying is that things change quickly in this world and not everyone is as trustworthy as they seem."

I sat there quietly and looked out at the ocean. Maybe Massimo was right. I had placed a lot of trust in Alessia, not knowing anything about her. So far, she hadn't given me a reason not to. She told me she would keep me safe from the Costas, and she did. She also said she would get in touch with Dante and that he would come, and now he was here. All I wanted to do was get back to New York and start our lives over. I didn't care anymore what I needed to do to make that happen. I'd get them back and then I'd kill my fucking cousin myself. The anger that had been boiling deep inside me was ready to be unleashed. I wouldn't have been in this mess if his greedy ass hadn't put me in harm's way. It was the envy of others that caused heartache in my life, and I was sick of it.

"They will be ready for you soon. Remember what I said about Alessia. If someone had warned me when I was young to only trust myself, then maybe my life would be different today."

I looked back at the man across from me. For someone who runs such a large family, you would think he wouldn't sound as if he had so many regrets. According to his sister, their reach in Sicily was vast. She spoke of their family's business and her brother as if she would prefer to have nothing to do with it. Now here he was, sounding just the same. It made me wonder if this life was something Dante had always desired. Maybe, like Alessia and Massimo, it was passed on to him and he made do with what he had. Growing up a Romano I always knew of the Corsettis, and then The Dark Kings. I never imagined what they had wasn't what they wanted, but also I had never asked.

CHAPTER THREE

DANTE

Today wasn't the first time we had entered the De Bartoli estate, but I sure as hell hoped it would be the last time. People speak of their family in ways that would terrify the strongest of men. As the largest family in Sicily, they controlled the entire island. They almost never left Italy and if they did, it was only for a short time. I knew Alessia as the insane sister of the mighty Massimo and only the people close to them knew the truth about their arrangement. Now we sat at a long hand-carved wood table overlooking the ocean waiting for her to come and state her demands. Demands I had expected, because even when we were all young, Alessia did nothing out of the kindness of her own heart.

"What a lucky girl I am today! Three gorgeous men all just waiting for me to join them," she said as she approached me.

"Alessia, always a pleasure," I said as I leaned in to kiss her cheek.

"Dante, you are such a sweet talker. It's never a pleasure for anyone to meet me, and you know that."

She moved to Ares next, greeted him and then stood back, staring at Nico in the corner. He refused to sit, and I wasn't about to make a scene. Alessia's men took our weapons at the door, so the knife he typically used to calm his nerves was gone.

"Nico, my love, don't I deserve a kiss?"

"Fuck off Alessia."

"Tsk, tsk, now is that any way to speak to your host?"

"Where is she?"

"Oh, she's here. No need to worry. I'll bring her to Dante shortly, but there is business we need to discuss first. Come, sit down."

I looked over at Nico in desperation. He needed to sit. We needed to comply until we had Valentina. When he finally took a step forward, I let go the breath I was holding in. I gave him a small nod and watched as he took his seat to my left.

"Very good. See, you can still follow orders, can't you, my pet?"

Nico flinched at her name for him but otherwise stayed quiet while Alessia took her seat.

"What can I have brought for you? Wine? Scotch? It's nearly dinner. I hope you will stay."

"I appreciate the offer, Alessia, but it's best if we get this over with. We need to get back to New York and handle a few things now that we know Valentina has been with you," I said, answering for all of us.

"So sweet isn't she?"

"Yes, she is."

"I asked her today to stay with me and she declined. You must have some sort of magic dick for her to deny me."

I didn't give in to her back-handed compliment. "What is it you want, Alessia? It's time for us to move this whole thing forward."

"Well, as you know, I saved your little one's life. So I think I deserve something in exchange."

"You didn't save her. You risked her by getting involved with the Costas," Nico ground out through clenched teeth.

"That's where you are wrong. I heard the news of the Costas moving on her and stepped in. It was the least I could do for my long-time friends."

Someone from their staff walked in with wine glasses and a platter of food. Alessia stopped talking to approve of the wine and waited while I tasted it as well.

"Very good. Please make sure my guests are never without," she instructed as she lifted her glass, "How about a toast? To the mysterious Valentina Romano and the men she's tamed with that delightful pussy of hers."

Nico made a move to stand, but stopped when I held my hand up to him. We drank and Alessia continued to talk in circles. Without giving me answers to any of the questions I asked. She got Nico so aggravated, he pushed back from the table and paced the room.

"What's wrong, my love? Impatient to see your latest piece of ass?"

"Shut the fuck up, Alessia. Just tell me what you want. You asked for me and I'm here. Stop with the fucking games already!" he yelled as he advanced on her. The men in the corners of the room all stepped forward but stopped when Alessia held her hand up, allowing Nico right into her personal space.

She leaned back in her chair, ignoring the fact he was so close to her he could snap her neck. "Oh fine. You don't have to get all emotional about it."

I watched as she reached forward and held her hand up to the side of his face. Nico's entire body tensed at her touch, but he closed his eyes and waited for her to go on.

"There, there, see. I always know what you need, don't I? Tell me, Nico, how has your life been since you nearly killed me and ran from my country?"

He stood up straight and her hand fell to her lap. "My life is nothing of your concern. Not anymore."

"That's where you are wrong. I want your life. All of it. If you want your little bitch to go home safely with Ares and Dante, then you are staying with me."

"Wait a minute," I interrupted before she could go any further, "This isn't some kind of trade. We have had a treaty in place for years, Alessia. By taking Valentina, you broke that treaty. I was willing to overlook it as a minor oversight since you agreed so easily to give her back, but Nico is not part of the negotiations."

She lifted her glass of wine to her lips without breaking eye contact with me. Nico went back to pacing the room and Ares was strangely quiet through this entire thing. He had his eyes focused on something in the courtyard and never really looked away.

"You were getting too big, Dante. Something needed to be done. The power your father had over that city of yours was impressive, but what you have gained since his death is just greedy. The treaty is void. I will not honor it. It was an agreement made by old, entitled men and it's not in my best interests to see it through. I'm sure you understand."

"I want to see her."

"Soon. She's not far," Valentina's eyes drifted over to Ares and her lips pulled up in a wicked smile, "But you know that already, don't you, pretty boy?"

Ares' eyes shifted to me, and he gave me a small nod. He had been watching Valentina the entire time. I should have known.

"Alessia, your brother and I have always had a good working relationship. When we were younger, you and I never had any problems. That should be reason enough for you not to be concerned with anything that happens in New York. It is my territory and you are here."

"I don't want to take over your city, Dante. I just want to know that I can if I feel like it."

This insane bitch was working my last nerve. I would never bow down to her and risk my people. She knew that. The problem was, half the time she was out of her mind and the other half she was destroying those around her.

"That will never happen and you know it. Rather than throwing aside an agreement that was made to protect both of our families, why don't we just renegotiate terms?"

She shook her head slowly. "Not good enough."

"Tell me why you want Nico, then."

"He's mine. He's always been mine and I want him back. My little pet could use some training. You've kept him well over the years, but it's time he came home."

"This is not my home," Nico growled back at her.

"But it was, once. Or did you already forget all the time we spent here? You had promised me the world, Nico, and now it's time you follow through on those promises."

Nico's face went pale. Alessia wasn't negotiating a thing. She was laying down the things she expected in return for Valentina. I looked over at Nico, but he couldn't pull his eyes from Alessia.

"Fine. I'll stay, but the treaty stays in place, and Valentina leaves with Dante."

My mind was screaming no, but Nico didn't need to say it out loud. We all knew which way this was heading. He had no choice but to stay, just in the same way I'd agree to dropping the treaty. We would all do anything to get Valentina back. Once we had her, then I could deal with the fallout. Her safety was our number one concern.

"If the treaty stays, then weaklings like the Costas will rise again and try to take over. You three can barely hold together your own city any more. Let me in and I'll protect you."

"No. We can rework terms, but the Corsetti Family will not be taking protection from you," I said, standing up from my seat.

"So you agree Nico stays?"

I looked at my brother. Leaving him here was not part of the plan, but Alessia's obsession with him had only grown in the years they had been apart.

"If he chooses to."

"I do."

"Fine. Bring Valentina here. We will meet again to discuss our next steps."

"Fun. Fun!" she sang out as she got to her feet and opened the door to the courtyard.

"Brother, bring the little beauty up to see her men!"

Now I knew why Ares couldn't stop staring. If Valentina had been with Massimo, then there was good reason to keep an eye on her. Alessia's brother put on a good front to the other families. The decision to let him be the face of their enterprise was a good business move, but on one drunken night when we were in our early twenties, he divulged too much information. He was bitter, resentful and likely the person who would murder his sister one day. As the only son to the De Bartolis, he had always assumed he would be the head of the family. When his father named his older sister, all hell broke loose. The only reason he had gotten as far as he had in this world was because of what happened between her and Nico.

The door opened and Massimo held it as Valentina stepped in. She looked amazing, and it was a relief to see she had been well taken care of. Instead of coming to me, or even Ares, she hurried across the room and lunged at Nico. He took a step back to catch her in his arms, and the pain in my chest at what he was about to do was unbearable. He held her tight as she cried in relief, his face was nuzzled into her neck and when he placed her back on her feet, he seemed to have been whispering something into her ear. She placed a kiss on his lips and took a step back. She came to both Ares and myself, and the feeling of her back in my arms calmed everything inside of me.

"I love you," she whispered into my ear, "I love you all so much."

She stepped back and stood next to me with her hand in mine.

"Alessia, I cannot thank you enough for the time you allowed me to spend here. You have taken such great care of me and I hope that someday you will visit us all in New York so I can show you the same hospitality."

Alessia stepped forward and held Valentina's face in her hands. "You are such a sweet girl. A wonderful woman and I have enjoyed your companionship, which is why this is harder than I had hoped."

"We will stay in touch, I promise."

"No, little beauty, that's not what I mean," Alessia turned to Nico, "Should I tell her, lover, or will you?"

CHAPTER FOUR

NICO

The way she looked at me made me want to wrap her up in blankets and carry her across the ocean in my arms. Valentina didn't deserve this. When she came to me first, I couldn't even breathe. It was the last thing I expected, but her words nearly broke me.

"I was so worried about you. I knew you would think the worst, and I had no way to tell you I was okay. I love you, Nico. I love you."

Those were words that would haunt me in my sleep. Now I stared at her as she flinched at Alessia's "lover" comment and all I could think about was how much worse this was going to get before it ever got better.

"Can we have a minute alone?"

"I don't think so."

"Alessia, please," I said and the look on Valentina's face was just as shocked at my use of the word please as it was with the new dynamic in the room.

"Fine." She stood making a show of twirling her dress around her body. Years ago, a movement like that would have me crawling to her on my knees, but now it was just another thing that made me sick. "I'll give you five minutes, then meet me in our bedroom."

Valentina let go of Dante's hand and stepped forward, "What do you mean —?"

"Oh, nothing dear, I'm sure your men can explain it well. Now let's say our goodbyes and remember, the offer still stands. I will always have a place for you by my side."

Alessia pulled Valentina into her arms and placed a kiss on either cheek. By the look on her face, Valentina was equal parts confused and angry. I couldn't blame her.

"Massimo, come. Let's give my pet and his men a moment alone. Dante, it's always a pleasure... and pretty boy ... I wouldn't mind having you by my side, either. Seriously Dante, where did you collect such beautiful specimens?" she asked as Ares turned his head and pulled his arm away from where she was trying to touch him.

When the door closed and it was only the four of us left, I was at a loss for words. I looked down to ensure my chest had not burst open with my lifeblood falling to the floor, because the pain was enough to believe it was true. I should have told her about my past. She deserved to know before this, but now I had mere minutes to help her understand what would happen next.

"Ragazzina, sit. Let us explain what will happen. Alessia is an impatient woman and won't wait long for Nico," Dante said, pointing to the door.

She took a seat next to him, but her eyes never left me. "What's going on?"

He reached for her chin and pulled her attention to him. "Nico is staying with Alessia. We will leave and head back to our home here on the island until I finish my business with the De Bartolis."

"Why would he stay here? Why would you stay here?" she asked, turning her attention back to me.

"It's what she wants, la mia bella ragazza. A simple trade, me for you."

She stood and walked to me, pushing Dante away as he tried to hold her back. "No. You aren't staying here. You're coming home with us. I don't care what she says, she can't just keep you."

"She can, and she will."

"No. Absolutely not. Why would she even want this, anyway? Unless... she loves you," Valentina said as her voice cracked with the realization of what was really going on, "And you love her. Do you love her, Nico?"

I couldn't face her. How couldn't I break her heart the way I needed to? She dropped to her knees in front of me and the dam broke. Her body shook with tears and I didn't know what else I could do. She needed to leave with Dante and Ares. She couldn't be here. It wasn't safe for her, and as much as I knew that, I wanted her to stay. She wrapped her arms around my legs and I could feel the sobs that shook her body as if they were my own.

"Yes, Valentina. I love her. I always have and I always will."

The words felt bitter on my tongue and burned through my gut. Ares got up and went to her, pulling her from me even as she continued to call my name. This was worse than I ever imagined. I knew I had fallen in love with her the minute we brought her home. When they took her, it only increased that need for her to complete me, but to see her like this, it almost made me believe what she said was true. When she whispered those words, "I love you," my heart wanted to believe it, but my mind told me I was a fool. It made sense for her to fall in love with Dante. She had planned for that her whole life, but to fall for me so quickly, no. It wasn't possible. I wasn't the type of man women fell in love with.

"Come, la mia piccola bambola. It's time for us to leave."

Ares held her close to his side as they turned and walked from the room. A part of me died when she didn't even bother to look back. The pain was unreal, worse than anything I had felt before in my life. It was even worse than the night I believed I had killed Alessia.

"Nico." Dante's voice pulled me from my thoughts. "You need to keep control of yourself. You know Alessia better than all of us. Be smart, not impulsive. She will expect the old you, not the person you've become. Do you understand?"

I stared at the door. I could hear him, but the words he said meant nothing to me now. "She will hate me."

"No, she loves you. There is no room for hate in her heart."

Dante turned and left. There were no promises of working everything out, nothing about how everything would be okay. He knew as well as I did that nothing good could come of my situation. After I did my best to calm the rage and devastation inside me, I made my way through the house and to Alessia's bedroom. I had spent nearly a year living with her when I was in my twenties, so it wasn't hard to find my way around. I rounded the corner to the master suite and was greeted by her asshole brother.

"Good to have you home, Nico."

"This isn't my home."

"Isn't it? I mean, if I remember correctly, your plans to marry my sister and rule my island with her were only thwarted by the fact that you nearly killed her. Now that you are back, I imagine I'll be asked to step down. She will want to make room at the table for her little pet."

I lunged at him and reached for his neck as I held him up against the nearest wall. "Don't start with me, Massimo. There are a lot of things that have changed over the last ten years. Don't underestimate me."

"Oh, the big bad Nico Marchesi is going to do what? Kill me? Go ahead, my sister will have you murdered in your sleep," he choked out as I tightened my hold.

"Boys! That's enough!" Alessia's voice ran through me like daggers of ice in my blood. "Nico, please put my brother down. He knows nothing other than his jealousy and it's enough to get him killed if he's not careful."

I let go of Massimo and watched as straightened his shirt and jacket. "You stupid, stupid girl. I told you he was going to be a problem."

I watched as he made his way past me and back down the hallway.

I turned back to Alessia. "We need to talk."

"There are a lot of things we need to do, my love, but talking isn't first on the list." She reached for me, but I took a step back. There was no way in hell I was going to let her get her claws back into me after all these years.

"If you want anything from me, then I need some answers first."

"Oh, fine. You are such a party pooper sometimes. Come, we'll talk on the portico. It's a beautiful night."

We got out to the patio that overlooked the ocean and for a brief minute, I remembered the good with Alessia. There wasn't much of it. We were a mess together. Hate, love, more hate. Our entire world revolved around each other and it was damaging to her family and to our hearts. Dante and Ares stayed in Sicily, refusing to leave for New York when I told them my plans to marry her. Lust blinded me at the time, and no one could talk any sense into me. I was pissed at them for not trusting me to make the right decision, for not accepting my love for Alessia. But in the end, when everything happened, they were the only people I could turn to.

I walked to the table and pulled her chair out for her, because that's what she would have expected of me. Dante was right, the De Bartolis didn't know the person I am now. They knew the kind, light-hearted man who loved Alessia for who she was, not what she had. The problem with that was Alessia turned out to be one crazy bitch.

We didn't bother with small talk. I didn't see the point. As soon as we sat, the staff from their kitchen brought out plates of food. Some of my favorites were there; pasta del mar, fried calamari. I looked across at Alessia to see her smiling, pleased with herself as usual.

"You remembered what I like."

"I remember everything about you, Nico. I could never forget all the things we shared, all the love we had. That's why I wanted you back. It's time for me to marry and start a family, which means I need you here, not playing with children in that dirty city of yours."

"Why didn't you come to me sooner? You realize I've thought you were dead for over ten years now."

"It wasn't time then. It's time now."

"So you let me just live with the guilt that I killed you?"

"Oh please, you didn't have any guilt. If you did, then you wouldn't have been running all over the city with your whores. You would have been mourning my death like a proper Italian man. But you didn't mourn me. You ran like a fucking little coward. That's why you didn't know I was alive. You didn't bother to stay around long enough to find out."

I picked up the glass of wine in front of me, and it took everything in my power not to throw it at her head.

"I wasn't a coward. I left because I wasn't ready to die. Your father would have killed me if I stayed. You know that."

"I never would have let him."

"You didn't have power over him. Not then."

"You always underestimated me, Nico. After everything I showed you, everything we did, you still think I'm the little girl who would go running to Daddy whenever some big dangerous man hurt her feelings. That's not who I am. You should know that by now. In this world on my island, when big evil men hurt me, I kill them."

"This was never the life you wanted."

"No, but it's what you wanted. I built all of this for us."

The words she was saying sounded insane, even to me. It was going to take longer than I had hoped to work my way out of this mess, which meant I needed to play to her wishes regardless of what it would do to me.

"If you had worked this hard for us, then why didn't you just come and find me? It's not like I've been hiding. You've known this whole time I've been with Dante. Why bother with Valentina when all you needed to do was tell me you were alive?"

"I'm not a fool. You would have turned me away. I've had people watching you for years, Nico. I've known every move you have made, and none of them led you back to me. As for Valentina? She was easy prey. But I have to admit it was a bit of a two birds and one stone situation. I knew how valuable she was to all of you, so if I took her from those fools, then I knew you'd come for her. The treaty needs to end. However, once I met your little girl, I could see the appeal. Her perfectly red lips, against her pale skin and dark hair, make her very desirable. I've never been one for petite women, but she has everything I'd ever want. I know you think I'm full of shit, but my offer to her was very real. If she wants to come here and be by our side, then I will have her. She was a delightful treat to have for the last couple of weeks."

There wasn't much more I could say to Alessia. She had already made her mind up about how things would go. I would just need to do what I could to keep my distance until Dante negotiated things in our favor. I picked up my fork and ate. The foods of my home country were ones I craved and longed for, but with today's events, it all tasted like sawdust. My mind wandered to my beautiful little girl. I said a silent prayer that Dante and Ares could console her. I knew them well enough to know they would lead her to believe it was my choice to leave her. The problem with that was when she found out the truth, she would hate us all.

CHAPTER FIVE

VALENTINA

"You have to eat."

"I'm not hungry," I mumbled as I rolled over and pulled the covers over my head. The last couple of weeks had been a disaster. I still wasn't over Nico breaking my heart with his awful words, and Dante spent more time at the De Bartolis than he did with Ares and I. We were falling apart before we even got started and that just wasn't fair.

"Please, la mia piccola bambola, you are wasting away. I can't stand the look in Dante's eyes when he sees you like this. We are worried about you. Please, just eat a little something." Ares begged every day for me to eat, sleep, shower. I didn't want to do any of it. I didn't want to do anything. The only time I felt relief was when Dante was inside me. Ares and I still hadn't taken that step in our relationship, and I was beginning to believe every lie my mind told me. That he didn't want me anymore. I was more of a burden than a help and I certainly wasn't desirable when I hadn't changed out of my sweatshirt in three days.

"Tell me what you need, please. I will give you the world. Just tell me."

My heart was broken, and it wasn't Ares' fault. It wasn't anyone's fault, but Nico's.

"I want to see him."

"We told you that's not a good idea. In fact, I don't even know if Alessia would agree to it."

"Then call him so I can talk to him on the phone. I want to hear his voice."

"No, my love. We can't do that."

I pulled the covers down so I could see him. "Why is everything up to her? I'm so tired of her. Alessia, this, Alessia, that. You are all so scared of her and it doesn't make any sense. She's nothing but a home wrecker who spends every moment of her day trying to prove she is man enough to run her family."

After the words left my mouth, I covered my hand. I sounded so petty and jealous, it was embarrassing. "I'm sorry. I didn't mean all that."

"It's fine, don't apologize. What you said was true."

"You and Dante keep telling me that Nico thought she was dead. I want to know why and how. He needs to tell me everything. I deserve that."

Ares got up and started pacing my room. He was losing patience with me and I couldn't blame him. The villa here in Sicily was something you'd see in the movies. It was all cobblestone walkways, open porticos, white linens and greenery. I loved everything about this property except for the fact that Nico wasn't here.

"You need a shower and I'm done listening to your poor me stories. Nico is gone. You have me and Dante. If we are not good enough for you, then you need to make that decision and leave us, but we will not sit around and let you curl up into a ball and die."

He approached my bed, pulled back the covers, and lifted me into his arms. The next thing I knew, he dumped me into a cold shower, fully dressed. I screamed as Ares laughed, pulling clothes from the both of us while the water warmed up.

"Not fair!"

"I'm done playing fair," he said as he yanked my soaking wet hoodie over my head, "I've been patient as a saint and now we are doing things my way."

The rest of my clothes were gone in an instant, as were Ares'. I couldn't pull my eyes from him. His body was completely covered in the most beautiful artwork I had ever seen in my life. Not to mention his huge fucking cock that was rock hard and calling for me. I stepped closer to him, reaching for it, but my distraction was pointless. He wasn't kidding when he said his way.

"Later." He pushed my hand away and turned me around, pulling my hair down from the messy bun it had lived in for days.

I stood there while he lathered my hair, washing it twice, and then he conditioned and brushed it to remove the tangles. One thing that was nice about having a boyfriend with long hair was he knew how to take care of mine. When he was done, he continued to wash my body as if I were incapable of doing anything myself. I drew the line when he decided he was going to shave my legs.

"Give me that," I said, holding my hand out for the razor, "I'm a grown woman who can shave her own legs."

"You sure about that?" he said, quirking a smile down at me.

I ignored him and finished what I needed to do while he washed himself up. I loved the showers here. Not only were they as large as the ones at home, but they also provided a view of the ocean. My favorite was the one outside in the garden. I was too miserable to enjoy it yet, but I imagined what it would be like under the water with Dante and Ares. Showering outside should be on everyone's bucket list. When we were done, he wrapped me in an oversized white towel and ushered me back to the bed.

"I need clothes."

"No, you don't."

Ares' towel dropped, and he was just as hard as he had been in the shower. My heart raced at the prospect of this finally being the moment I'd waited for and then just as quickly as the excitement rose, it was ruined by a slow shake of his head.

"Not yet."

"Not yet, or not ever?"

"What are you talking about?"

"I don't know. It just seems like you're punishing me. I want you, Ares, but you don't seem to want me in the same way."

He crawled up the bed to me and pulled me into his side. "You are so very wrong, my little doll. I'm sorry if I made you feel that way. I want you more than I've wanted anything in my whole life. Tonight, I will show you that, but not until you eat.

I had been holding my breath in fear, maybe excitement. I couldn't tell which. But then he layered another condition on us being together... food.

I sat up and leaned over to the nightstand where he had left a plate of meats, cheese, bread, and fruit. I broke the bread open and stuffed it with everything but the fruit. Then, like an animal, I stuffed nearly the whole thing in my mouth.

"MmmHowmmm. ... bout... hmmhmm.... now?" I mumbled through chewing the massively large bite I took.

Ares was laughing so hard he snorted as he pulled the food from me. "What is the matter with you? You are going to choke to death and then I'll never get to fuck you."

That was the wrong thing to say because I laughed and proceeded to spit out half the food in my mouth. It felt good to laugh. Over the last couple of weeks, I wondered if I'd ever laugh again. I missed Nico. It felt like a piece of my heart was missing, but Ares was right. I still had him and Dante, and they deserved more from me. Once we cleaned up the mess, Ares fed me the rest of the food on the plate like he had the first time he brought me a meal. It felt like years ago when all that had happened, but in truth, it was only a couple of months ago.

He reached over me and placed the plate on the nightstand. Sitting there naked, eating with a man as gorgeous as Ares was nearly impossible. I wanted him so badly but

I didn't know how to make the first move. This was all so new to me, and yet it was Ares. He held a place in my heart, just the same as Dante and Nico.

"I'm sorry. You deserve more from me," I said, looking up at him.

"Please don't apologize. I'm the one who caused this crater between the two of us. At first, it was because I didn't want to take that step with you until you knew the whole truth. Now, with Nico gone, I didn't want to force myself on you. I have no idea what our future will hold, La mia piccola bambola. The only thing I know is that a world without your smile isn't a world I want to be in."

I wanted to make fun of him for being so corny, but I couldn't. He was telling me the truth. I could see it in his eyes. I know he missed Nico, too. They were best friends for their entire life. I had been selfish, and it wasn't right.

"We have all come a long way in a very short time. Trust is growing, but it's hard. Especially for me now that I know there was never room for me in Nico's heart."

Ares reached for me and pulled me to his chest. He rubbed gentle circles into my lower back as I fought back another round of tears. "Don't think that way. Nico loves you in his own way. Things are just complicated right now, but we will work it all out. We will be okay Valentina, I promise."

"I know we will." I lifted my head from his chest and reached up to kiss him. What I had planned to be a gentle reassuring kiss was fire the second our lips connected. Ares' hand came around the back of my head as he held me to him. His tongue forced its way into me, darting in and twirling around in a way that made my insides tingle. My hips thrust forward, and I ground my pelvis into him, only to be flipped over onto my back as his body covered mine.

"You're sure?" he questioned, looking down at me, "Because once we start, this will never end."

"Yes. I'm sure. I love you, Ares."

He closed his eyes as my words sunk in. I let my fingers wander down his biceps and trace along the spectacular tattoos there. They were remarkable.

"You're so beautiful," I whispered.

Ares' head dropped to my neck, and he sucked at the delicate skin there as he lifted my leg and aligned himself with my opening. Dante, Ares and Nico were all so different, it made sense they would feel different. He didn't waste any time, with one thrust he entered me, and my body pulled him in as if it were meant to be. I cried out in shock and wrapped my legs around him. He didn't move again until I had adjusted, but once he did, I saw stars. I always imagined Ares would be my gentle lover. That's the side of him I always saw when we were with Dante and Nico, but tonight, he fucked me with abandon. His movements were harsh and deliberate, like a starved man who finally got what he had been waiting for.

My orgasm hit me so fast it shocked the both of us. I moaned in pleasure as he hit that spot deep within me at every thrust until my body had had enough and pulled me over the deep end with no warning. My inner walls trembled and held him tight as my body burned with pleasure. I screamed out his name as he ground his hips forward, never letting up even as I was falling into a deep oblivion.

"Fuck, that's so hot. I can't believe you're mine," he said as my body went weak and his mouth descended on me, "I want more."

Whatever that man wanted, I would give him. He rolled us over in one fluid movement until I was straddling him.

"Move for me, La mia piccola bambola."

My body still was in shock over what it had just experienced, but the look on Ares' face wasn't one I would deny. Slowly, I rocked myself forward, only to be met with his fingers on my clit. I pulled back quickly, trying to save my over-sensitized bud. Yet he wouldn't stand for it.

"Don't pull away from me. I want more. Now."

His large hand came over my hip as he encouraged me to move the way he wanted me to. I was so wet and relaxed that the only way I could keep my pace was holding onto Ares for dear life. I arched my back and reached behind me, thrusting my hips forward as he tortured my clit and told me all the things he loved about me.

"So gorgeous, yes, just like that, my little doll. Look at those tits. Fuck, I want to suck on them."

Suddenly, he sat up, and his arms came around me. Before I knew it, his mouth covered my breast and the sucking motion brought my slowly moving climax forward in a rush.

"I... I can't wait... Ares, I need to come."

"Let me see it. Give it to me, Valentina."

I cried out as my second climax hit me before the true after-effects of the last one had even left my body. I was done, broken down and completely lifeless, yet Ares still hadn't finished. Even sitting astride him was too much for me to maintain. My chest fell forward onto his and my head rested under his neck.

"I'm sorry... I just don't think I can move right now."

Ares let out a deep, throaty laugh as his cock twitched inside of me. "Perfect."

He held me to him and thrust up from underneath me. I wish I could say I made some effort to help things along, but I couldn't even lift my arms. He held me tight and continued to fuck me. Each thrust was accentuated by a deep grunt that vibrated his chest until finally his body gave in to the climax he had been chasing. His body tensed under me as I felt him explode inside of me. His deep thrusts slowed until finally he laid back on the bed, pulling me down with him.

"Ti amo mia piccola bambola."

CHAPTER SIX

DANTE

I was so fucking sick of Alessia De Bartoli that I was highly considering just killing her and moving on. If it was a suicide mission, then I would have already done it. If not for me, then Nico. He was holding on by a string, worried sick about Valentina and no matter how many times I told him she would be okay, he refused to believe me. To be honest, I wouldn't have believed me either. Alessia was in full on wedding planning mode, since Nico told her he wouldn't sleep with her until after the ceremony. I didn't think she'd go for it, but he was putting on quite a show while he had been there. The night he told me she agreed, I thought he was lying, but sure enough, she was bragging about being a born-again virgin for her wedding night when I arrived the next morning.

Massimo wasn't much help either. He didn't want Nico there any more than Nico wanted to be there, but whenever we were meeting to hash out a new agreement, he would side with his sister's wishes. I was running out of options. There wasn't much I had left to offer her, and I wasn't giving up my city. Nico didn't even want that.

I walked into the house in search of a drink. It was quiet, and the lights were out, but not that late. I made my way back to the bedrooms, assuming I'd find Valentina curled up under the covers, since she was basically living in bed, but she wasn't there. Panic set in as I moved through her room to her bathroom and still I couldn't find her. As I moved down the hallway toward Ares' room, I heard a shout that made my heart stop. Was she hurt? I ran toward the sound of her voice and burst into my bathroom.

"What the fuck?" I choked out at the sight of things.

Ares was naked as the day he was born in my tub with Valentina bouncing up and down on his dick. "Are you kidding me right now? The way she screamed, I thought she was hurt."

Valentina only smiled and reached a hand out for me as Ares laughed, "What can I say? She likes a little pain with her pleasure, but you already know that."

I adjusted myself because my pants were suddenly way tighter than they were supposed to be. "Well, it's good to see you two have moved on from whatever the fuck was bothering you."

I turned to leave, but stopped when she called for me. "I need you too," she panted as Ares' movements never quit.

I looked back at them, and her eyes hadn't left me. Ares had a shit-eating grin on his face as his eyebrows rose. Fuck. I wasn't walking away now. I knocked back the rest of my scotch and put the glass on the counter. It didn't take long for me to strip out of my clothes, and I reached for Valentina as soon as I got into the warm water.

"Give her to me. You've had her all day."

Valentina smiled as Ares complied. My sweet girl let me pull her through the water and climbed atop of me without a second thought. The moment her warm center enveloped my cock, every worry I had escaped me.

"That's a good girl," I said as I watched her close her eyes and smile at my praise. Ares grabbed his cock and was jerking himself off as he watched her rise and fall in the water. Her body was warm, supple and mine for the taking. I had fucked her every night since Nico left, but this time, something felt different. She seemed lighter, as if she had let go some of the stress that was bogging her down all this time.

Ares moved through the water and sat next to me, pushing Valentina closer to my chest. She complied without hesitation. When she leaned forward, he reached for the tight rosebud that we had only played with until this point. Her whimpers of need were unmistakable. She wanted this and more.

"Do you like it when Ares plays with your tight little hole, Ragazzina?"

"Yes."

"Does it feel good?"

"Fuck yes."

"How good?"

"So damn good, sir... so damn good."

"Is this enough, or do you need more?"

She looked up at me, then back at Ares before she whispered, "I think I'm ready."

I pressed my lips to hers, grateful for everything she had given us. "Come on then, let's get dried off."

Valentina took two towels from the rack and handed one to me and one to Ares. Her movements were quick, and she kept gazing at us both while we dried off and made our way into my bedroom.

"Was there something wrong with your bath?" I asked Ares as Valentina propped herself up on the bed.

"No, I just knew you would be home soon and yours is bigger than mine."

I nodded my head and smiled as he gave me one of his signature Ares winks.

Valentina's nervous voice pulled my attention back to her. "What should I do? Is this okay? Do you want me somewhere else?"

"Take a deep breath Valentina, you will be just fine. Ares will get you comfortable while I get everything we need."

She nodded her head, and I turned back to the bathroom to get a fresh towel and a bottle of lube. The excitement that ran through me felt as if Ares had wrapped me in his electro-conducted ropes and I couldn't break free. A tingle ran over my skin and my heart beat rapidly. I hurried my way back to Valentina to find her more than relaxed with Ares between her thighs, sucking on her clit.

"See now, that's much better." I said as I crawled into bed next to her, "Come here, my pretty girl."

I reached for her as Ares moved next to us. "Do you want me to explain what we are going to do?"

"Please."

"We will take things slow. Ares is going to sit up against the headboard and you will fuck him as you have been... all day. Slowly, though, nothing too rushed. Once you are comfortable, I will stretch you as I have before. Only with my fingers at first, then when you are relaxed, I will enter you from behind."

"Okay. I can do this."

"Yes, you can, and once you do, I promise you will love it. We will make sure you are taken care of, Ragazzina."

"I know, I'm ready. I'm nervous, but I've wanted this for a while now."

"Just remember your numbers. If you want us to stop, what do you do?"

"Five, I say five. But I will warn you first with a four or a three."

"Very good."

Ares reached for Valentina, and she went willingly. I watched as he kissed her softly, massaging her breasts and whispering sweet words into her ear. When his mouth traveled to her neck, she lifted herself over him and reached for his cock, lining him up and lowering herself onto him.

"Damn. You feel so good."

She rocked her hips slowly, moving at what would have been a torturous speed had they not been at it all day. I moved to reach for the lube and coated two fingers with it. Ares pulled her forward into his embrace and covered her mouth with his. The distraction worked to my advantage, and I pressed both fingers into her slowly. She groaned at the intrusion, but pushed herself back into me. I worked her slowly, stretching her to prepare her for my cock. Her movements continued and her breathing increased. She was getting close, and I wasn't ready for her to come yet.

I needed to be in that tight ass of hers when her cunt clenched down on Ares' cock.

"Not yet, my love. You will wait for us."

She whimpered and slowed her movements, trying to control her impending climax as I covered myself in lube and lined up with her tight little hole.

"Relax, my little doll. Breathe deeply and the first bit of pain will only last a second," he said as he ran his hands down her sides.

She nodded her head as I spread her cheeks and slowly worked my way into her. It was the best and worst kind of torture, and it took all the control I had not to slam into her with all my force. Her body tensed, but once I was completely in place, she slowly started to relax. Ares' fingers disappeared between the two of them and he began stroking her clit. Before long, she shifted forward and slowly back, testing herself.

"Fuck, you are so tight, baby girl. Tell me where you are."

"A two, I'm a two. I'm good, really good," she said with a small laugh that lit up Ares' face.

We worked together, rocking forward and back, pushing and pulling, reaching for the high that only Valentina could provide us. Her breathing was labored and I could see in Ares' face he was holding on, waiting for her as I was.

"That's it, very good. You are such a good girl," I encouraged her as we picked up our pace.

"Please... please let me... sir, I can't hold on much longer."

She was there, and her begging did nothing but increase my own climb to that wave of pure unadulterated pleasure. I looked over her at Ares and he gave me a quick nod. "Now, Ragazzina. Give it to us now."

She cried out as her body shook between us. Her head fell to Ares' chest, and he grunted as he exploded into the tightened space of her hot cunt. With just a few more long and deep strokes, my own wave of desire made its way through my body and I yanked her up by her hair holding her tightly to me as I emptied myself into her tight ass.

"Fuck."

Ares reached for her as I let her go, and she wrapped her arms around him tightly. We stayed utterly still for a moment while each of us tried desperately to catch our breath.

"That was... amazing," she breathed out as I carefully pulled myself from her.

"Yes, that it was," Ares said, stroking her hair as I moved to clean up.

Some days I wonder how life got so hard, so fast. When my father died, I was young. I hadn't been prepared for everything it would take to keep the business running. I held out hope that it would all work itself out, and I held out hope for Valentina. Even when we were young, I knew she would be the perfect partner. It was only within the last few days I realized my feelings for her had moved from respect for the woman I'd marry, to love. Some part of me hated it. The risks she would face because she meant so much to us were monumental. The thought that people could harm her because they wanted to get to us kept me up at night. It was another thing I worried about, on top of all the drama with the Costas and the De Bartolis. When we finally make our way back to New York, things need to change. I needed to schedule a meeting with the other families. It was time they understood their role in our arrangement went beyond my protection and their place at my table. If they wanted to continue our partnerships, then threats like the Costas needed to be extinguished long before they got to me and my family.

I went back to Ares and Valentina and found them just as I had left them. I took a towel and cleaned our little girl up the best I could, then lifted her into my arms and back into the bathroom. I sat her in the oversized shower and started the water. It was early evening, but all I wanted was a warm shower, a change of clothes, and the rest of the night in bed with my woman.

"Is Nico okay?" she asked as I ran a soapy washcloth over her body.

"He is."

"I miss him."

"I know you do. It will get better in time."

"I want to see him, but Ares said no."

"I agree with him, this isn't a good time for you to go there. Things are complicated right now, and I need Alessia on our side, not only for your safety but for Nico's too."

"She wouldn't hurt him would she?"

I thought about it for a moment. The hurt Alessia left Nico with last time was psychological. I know Valentina was asking about physical threats but that wasn't the scariest part about him being there. Alessia was smart and manipulative. She was also a bit mad. Her highs and lows were dizzying, which was why it'd been so hard to negotiate peace with her. One day we would make progress and the next she would disagree.

"Physically? No. She may try but he has too much to live for now."

"What do you mean? I thought being with her was everything he ever wanted."

"He didn't say that to you though, did he?"

"He said he loved her, that he always had."

"It would do you well not to make assumptions of his situation. Nico's past is very complex and Alessia was a big part of it."

"Why can't you just tell me what happened? If I can't see him then I want to know the truth."

I turned the water off and reached for fresh towels. Valentina was quiet while I dried her off and helped her dress. By the time we made it back into my room, Ares was gone.

"Lay down, I'm going to get some water and food for you to snack on."

When I got to the kitchen, I grabbed some fresh fruit and cheese. I had no idea if she had eaten today since she hadn't really been functioning over the last couple of weeks.

Ares came in and grabbed a bottle of water.

"I'm grabbing her some food. Do you want anything?"

"Yeah, I was going to get something for us too. She ate earlier. A whole meal and a few snacks."

"It's about time."

"All it took was me offering her my dick as a reward, I'm kind of pissed I didn't think of it sooner," Ares said with a laugh, "How was he today?"

"Fine. I think. Alessia is planning their fucking wedding. She's gone straight off the deep end."

"Nico told me years ago she struggled with mental illness. Maybe she's just in the middle of a manic state and it will calm down once it slows."

"It's possible, but it's making her extremely difficult to work with. He told me yesterday that she spends the nights pacing the halls of the house, talking to herself. The longer he is there, the more she is breaking him down. He loves Valentina. I have no question about that, but he loved Alessia once. What he sees in her is breaking his heart. He never wanted a life like this for her, with or without him."

"So what do we do? Because Valentina is going to lose her shit when she realizes we have been lying to her. All she asked us for was honesty, and at the first sign of trouble, we are already feeding her lines of bullshit."

"Keep things very general with her, no specifics. As of right now I haven't actually lied to her. When she asks questions I don't want to answer I distract her. Nico is the one who lied but he did it to protect her. She will understand, but only if we can get him back."

"She wants to see him."

"I know, she told me."

"What did you say?"

"The same thing you did. I told her no and that the timing wasn't right."

"She won't stand for that answer much longer. Something shifted in her today, I can sense the fight in her again."

"I know, I felt it too."

"What are we going to do? I can only keep her distracted with my dick for so long."

I looked over at Ares and shook my head, "I've been thinking of having you take her home."

"To New York? She'd never agree."

"It's not really up to her, is it?"

CHAPTER SEVEN

ARES

Dante had left before Valentina and I had even considered waking up this morning. I loved that she enjoyed sleeping in as much as I did. Waking up with her in my arms every morning was like a dream come true. But now it was the middle of the afternoon, and she was standing across from me with her hands on her hips and a look of hatred on her face.

"No, I'm not going. This is bullshit. I told you all that I would stay if you didn't keep things from me and I know you all are keeping things from me. Now you want to take me back to New York? Without Dante? Without Nico? No, absolutely not."

I ran my fingers through my hair as she paced in front of me. Her arms were flailing around like a chicken and she was making such a fuss I was tempted to take her over my knee like Dante would if he were here.

"Why are you so disobedient?"

"Maybe because you are such an ass!"

"I don't understand why I am the one getting blamed here. It's not like I made this decision on my own."

"Well, if he was here, then I would yell at Dante, too."

"You absolutely would not be yelling at him. He would gag and flog you until you cried."

That comment earned me another dirty look.

"Listen, it doesn't make sense for us to stay here. The risks are too great, and we need to get back to check on the businesses."

"Like there aren't any risks in New York? I heard you and Dante talking the other night. Angelo is out of jail, isn't he?"

I shook my head. This woman was always spying on us. Serves Dante right. She was very clear she wanted to know everything, and we spent more time keeping things from her than telling her the truth.

"He is. But not for long."

"What is that supposed to mean?"

"Nothing. Listen, can we please just get some things packed up? The plane has been waiting for over an hour."

"No. I'm not going until I see Nico." She threw herself into the chair across from me and damn it if her breasts didn't look amazing while she had her arms crossed.

"If I take you to him, will you go?"

The hopeful look on her face was about to break me. "Yes. I just want to say goodbye. He owes me that much."

I stood and walked to the front hallway. She ran behind me as I descended the steps and got into one of our cars out front. Her body was buzzing with excitement, and she kept looking over at me as if she couldn't believe I was giving in. To be fair, I couldn't believe what I was doing either. Dante was going to kill me when we showed up. I had no idea what things looked like over there. I hadn't been back with him since we got Valentina, which meant he was solely responsible for working things out with Alessia. It wasn't how we liked to handle business, but until things settled down, neither of us were willing to let Valentina out of our sight.

I pulled up to the guard and lowered my sunglasses. "I'm here for Nico."

The guard nodded his head and opened the gates. I don't know why, but I assumed it would be harder to get in this place, especially with Valentina by my side. We got to the front and were taken into a sitting room just to the right of the main entrance as soon as we were let in. I had hoped we were waiting for Nico, but when Massimo made his way into the room, my easy go of it all ended.

"I hear you came for Nico?"

"We won't be long. I'm taking Valentina home this afternoon and she just wants a minute to say goodbye."

"I see. Does my sister know?"

"No, we just now decided to come."

"She's in with Dante."

"And Nico?"

"He's around, but I'd like to talk to you first."

"Then talk."

Massimo moved through the room and took a seat on the couch opposite ours. Valentina was behaving, thank fuck for that, and other than her hand clenching and unclenching my thigh, she was showing no signs of concern.

"It's time for Nico to leave," Massimo said.

"I couldn't agree with you more."

"My sister is... how do you say?...struggling right now. His presence is making things harder for her, yet she will never admit it."

"And what would you like me to do about it?"

"If you are taking Valentina home, then I want Nico to leave as well. Dante can stay and work things out with Alessia, but this wedding cannot go on."

"Wedding? What wedding?" Valentina went to stand, but I pulled her back to me.

"Alessia and Nico's wedding, of course. It cannot happen. The only way to stop it is to take him from here."

"How do you know she won't come after him?" I asked, as I held tight to Valentina's hand.

"She won't. She's too afraid of being rejected by him, by anyone really. That was why she took your little doll. She needed leverage to keep him."

"But you said..."

"Shhh, little love," I quieted Valentina before I lost the one good lead we had in weeks.

"How do you suppose we accomplish this?"

"I'll bring Nico to you now. He will leave with you if I tell him Alessia agreed."

"He knows her too well to believe that."

"I hear them up at night arguing. I know the things she has said to him, what her true desires are. It's not Nico, it's a husband and a family. She doesn't care who fills the role as long as someone does. There is pressure from the other families that neither of us are married. We do not have an heir and they are concerned. Although they see me as the don, she believes she can step into the spotlight and claim her title if she has a son."

No wonder she wanted Nico. He was the safe choice. A man she knew loved her was a better option than one she didn't know. "She doesn't have any other prospects."

"Sure, there are many. But none that she will trust."

"Bring him to me so I can speak with him. Dante doesn't even know we are here. I'll need a few minutes to send him a message."

"I understand."

This wasn't the way we normally handled things. Sure, any of us could make decisions to benefit the family in New York, but something as big as negotiating with the De Bartoli's was usually handled with Dante involved.

Ares: We are here. I brought Valentina to say goodbye to Nico, and before you lose your shit, read this entire message. Massimo is bringing me Nico to take him with me. He has agreed to let him go, that it's best for Alessia if he is out of the picture.

Dante: I'm assuming she doesn't know any of this.

Ares: No. I will leave with Nico and Valentina, and you will have to make your way out as if you know nothing. Massimo will handle his sister.

Dante: She will rain hell down on New York.

Ares: I think I have a plan for that. I'll explain it when I see you tonight.

Dante: Don't fuck this up.

I put my phone back in my pocket just as Nico walked into the room. I wasn't close enough to hold Valentina back, and she ran to him and threw herself into his arms.

"I don't care what you said. I don't care if you don't love me or can't love me... just please agree to come home."

He held her tight as he looked over at me with questioning eyes.

"What are you talking about?" he finally asked as he put her down.

"Massimo is letting you go. We need to leave now, though. There is a lot to discuss," I told him.

For once in our lives, Nico followed my instructions without question. He reached for Valentina's hand and pulled her from the room and towards the door, passing Massimo along the way.

"I've called the guard. You won't be stopped on the way out. And Nico? Try to stay out of Sicily for a while."

"Yeah, no problem."

We made our way through the front of the house and as Nico reached for the door, I heard the one sound that could ruin everything. Alessia's laughter as she came down the hallway hit me like a bag of bricks. I could hear Dante trying to keep her where she was, but their voices continued to get louder. There was no point in running and Nico realized it, too.

"Valentina! My little love! Have you come back for me?" Alessia said as she approached and pulled Valentina into her arms.

"No, I haven't. I'm here for Nico."

"Oh, silly child, you know Nico belongs to me. He isn't going anywhere."

Everyone was quiet, not even Massimo opened his big ass mouth. Valentina stepped forward until she was inches from Alessia's face.

"I trusted you. You took what was mine after I called you a friend. I'm sick of people taking what's mine and I'm here to take him back."

She turned her back and walked towards Nico, who held a hand out for her.

"No! No! No! You don't get to have him! He was mine, he was always mine."

Alessia moved in Valentina's direction and before any of us could do a thing. I watched as Valentina reached behind Nico and pulled a gun from his back. It was pointed right between Alessia's eyes in a matter of seconds.

"Don't point a gun unless you are ready to kill. That's what they taught me. Don't take the safety off unless you want to pull the trigger." I watched as she released the safety without even blinking.

"Do you want to know what else they taught me, Alessia? They taught me not to trust anyone. So unless you want to die without ever giving birth to that baby boy you dream of, back the fuck off."

Alessia held her hands up and took two steps back. Tears came to her eyes as she looked at Valentina. "I don't have anyone else."

"That's not my problem."

"You have no idea how hard it is being a woman with this much power. They underestimate me at every turn. I need a son to leave everything, too. I need a boy of my own to teach."

Valentina lowered the gun, put the safety back on it, and handed it to Nico. Then she did the one thing that no one would have expected and she reached out to Alessia and pulled her into her arms as the woman began to cry.

"I can't imagine how hard it is for you, but you know in your heart this is not the way."

Valentina ran her hands through her hair and down her back to soothe her. "It will get better. I promise. If we can help you, we will. But let us be friends, not enemies."

I exchanged glances with Dante and Nico, but it was Massimo who spoke up first, "Maybe we should give them a minute."

I looked back at Dante, and he nodded his head in the direction of the living room. Nico seemed hesitant to leave them, but followed when Dante called out his name.

"Well, that was certainly a turn of events," Massimo said as he moved through the room.

"It was," Dante said as he tapped his fingers along the side of the couch he was sitting at.

"I would apologize for my sister's behavior, but you all know she can be difficult."

Nico was still hovering in the doorway, keeping an eye on the girls. "You don't give her enough credit. She is a remarkable woman. She's just not the woman for me. Alessia needs help, Massimo. When I leave, you need to find her someone to work through all of this."

"It's hard. There is so much of our life that she cannot share with others, so speaking to a stranger isn't an option. For the last few years, she's spoken to me about it less and less."

"I may know someone," I said, "He's from New York. I will talk to him and see if he would come and spend a few months out here. He can be trusted."

"He will need to understand that if he breaks confidentiality, then I will kill him."

"Yeah, I know."

"We'll stay in town for the next few days, but after that, I need to get back to the city and handle things there. I think Nico and Valentina need some time before we walk back into that shit storm. Can I have an agreement from you that our original treaty stands?" Dante asked, turning to Massimo.

"Yes. For now. Alessia will need to comply until I can get her some help. Once she is doing better, we will meet again. She is right about a few things. The agreements made by our fathers when we were young don't all apply to us anymore."

"I agree."

"Ares, when do you think you will have an answer from your contact?"

"He's a psychologist with his own practice. I will know right away if he agrees, but he will need to make arrangements for his other patients."

"How do you know him?"

"He's a client from the shop. I'll be in touch when I speak with him."

Alessia and Valentina walked in holding hands. "I think we have come to a decision that may affect all of us. I've invited Alessia to come to New York and stay for a few months, and she agreed. We will wait until everything with the Costas and my cousin is settled, but after that, she is coming."

"With us?" Dante's eyebrows raised as he looked in her direction.

"Yes, with us. She needs people she can count on, and I consider her a friend. Even after everything that has happened."

I could see Dante's mind running through a million thoughts. Valentina had over-stepped but he wouldn't mention it here. I grinned to myself realizing that she just set herself up for the perfect punishment.

"Very well then. This may make things easier for your friend, Ares," Massimo said, turning back to me.

"It will."

Nico made his way over to Alessia. "I'm going to go now. I need to be with Valentina. You understand that, right?"

"I do. I'm sorry for all the trouble I've caused."

Nico pulled her into a hug, and she never let go of Valentina's hand. There was something between the two of them that seemed more than an ordinary friendship. Although given the similarities of how they were both raised, I suppose that made sense. I stood and gestured to Dante.

"Let's get going. I'll let Nico take my car back with Valentina and I'll ride with you."

"Thank you, sweet girl," Alessia said, placing a kiss on Valentina's cheek, "I will see you all soon."

We made our way back out the front of the house. Nico hadn't even looked back once he helped Valentina in the car. They drove off and a sense of relief came over me. I didn't want to be optimistic, but for the first time in a while, it felt as if we had made a step in the right direction.

CHAPTER EIGHT

NICO

I closed the car door and couldn't get off the De Bartolis property fast enough. I was finally leaving and with Valentina at my side. The last couple of weeks had been torture without her. It wasn't only missing her, it was keeping up the charade of being a person I hadn't been in years. My life had changed so much and anytime Alessia would see signs of me being anything other than the person she remembered, she would start questioning me. I loved her once. She was my entire world, but the things that pulled us apart were unforgivable. I know a lot of people who had thought they were in love when they were younger, but when they found their soulmate, they realized it wasn't love. This wasn't how it had been for me. I loved Alessia back then. I love Valentina now. They may be the two great loves of my life, but Valentina was my focus now. She was my world. My heart bled for Alessia. To see her in such a state was upsetting, but there wasn't much I could do to help. Marrying her was never an option. Valentina held my heart.

I looked over at her in the passenger's seat. She was looking out the window with a lost look on her face as I reached for her hand and refocused on the road. I had so much to tell her, and I prayed she would forgive me for everything that happened. My little beauty was more fierce than any of us had expected. When she pulled my gun out and pointed it at Alessia, I swear my heart had stopped. My black, cold, beaten heart that was just now on the path to recovery had stopped dead in my chest. Valentina had a heart of gold. There was no question about that. We took her from her home, told her she would need to accept us all to stay and endangered her life. Even after all that, she was willing to fight for us. Fight for me.

I pulled up to our villa and walked around the car to open her door. I reached for her and relished in the feel of her hand in mine. Everything about her made my body respond.

"Can we talk?" I asked before we moved to go into the house.

"I think we should. Dante and Ares won't be far behind us. I've been staying in your room. We can talk there."

She was staying in my room, even after everything that had happened. She chose my space over an empty guest room or staying with one of the guys. We made our way through the house, and the second I stepped into my room, I smiled. It smelled of her. The sweet vanilla body wash and lotion I had grown to love permeated the space, and I couldn't get enough of it.

"Why did you choose my room?"

"I don't know, really. I guess deep down I didn't want to be far from you. I didn't want to believe what you told me was true."

I unbuttoned my shirt and walked toward my closet. The constant need to be dressed up for Alessia was finally over, and I needed my clothes. Valentina sat on the edge of the bed while I changed. Her eyes on me made me want her more than ever, but I knew stripping her down and fucking her right now wouldn't have been a good move. She needed answers.

"I want to tell you everything. I should never have kept it all from you, but I thought this was all behind me. I never would have expected that any of this would happen. As far as I knew, Alessia was dead."

"Maybe start there, because I don't understand how that's even possible."

"I need to start at the beginning. When we were in our twenties, Dante's father sent the three of us here to Sicily to take care of some issues. It was a test of sorts, kind of a way to see if we were really ready for what was coming. The De Bartolis were in a war with another family here on the island and Mr. Corsetti had offered to send some men to help. Dante's father and Alessia's father had known each other when they were boys. Long before Mr. Corsetti ever moved to the States. Alessia's father had helped him gain his reputation in New York and until the day he died, he credited that man for a lot of his success. We couldn't fuck things up. It wasn't an option."

Valentina sat quietly, with no indication of what she was thinking.

"I didn't expect to meet Alessia. I knew Mr. De Bartoli had a son, but I never knew he had a daughter. We got involved shortly after Dante, Ares, and I arrived. I was a different person then. I was young and ignorant. I thought we had forever together, but that just wasn't the case. When the work here was done, I told Dante I was going to stay. I had planned to marry Alessia and work for her family. Even then, Massimo had suspected her father would leave the business to her and it was causing problems between the siblings. When her father announced it would be hers, Massimo lost his shit, but I stayed by her side. I proved to her she could be the woman she needed to be to run the family. Alessia felt if she were married it would make things easier and to this day, she still feels the only way to be successful is with a husband and a child."

"So what led to you think she had died?"

"I didn't just think she had died. I thought I had killed her."

Valentina's eyes went wide, and she reached for my hand. Even after so many years, this wasn't an easy story to tell.

"I'm sure you know by now that Dante, Ares and I have particular desires in the bedroom. Most of them we haven't even been able to share with you yet."

"Like what?"

"Dante is pretty simple to understand. You figured him out right away. He's a dom who likes having a little someone to take care of and punish in equal measure. Ares' and my kinks are a bit more dangerous."

"Like your knives?"

"Yes. My knives are more than a play toy. They are an extension of who I am. I know that you have cut yourself in the past and at some point, I'm going to want to know more about that. For me, the desire comes with the blood. Cutting you, watching you bleed, tasting it, everything we did that night were parts of the perfect fantasy. Sure, there are lots of things that go along with that, but for me, it's one of my biggest desires. It's more than just a want, it's become something I need out of a relationship."

"I see."

"Does that scare you?"

"No."

I nodded my head slowly but continued, "Alessia was the one who helped me understand these things about me. She wanted to experiment with all sorts of things, and we did. Regularly. I learned things I like, things I don't. I learned about my boundaries and the importance of communication, but I also learned how dangerous it all is. A lot of the reasons I prefer a relationship with Dante and Ares is so that what happened in Sicily can't ever happen again. With other partners in the room, they can help the more dangerous scenes stay on track."

"Scenes?"

"It's a term for play. We will get there some day. The way it would work is the four of us would sit down and discuss what we want out of play. You could choose things like what toys you would want to play with, how we would play with them and even for how long. Right now we have been making a lot of those decisions for you, but that will need to change as things progress between us."

"There is so much I still don't know."

"My beautiful girl, we will teach you."

She smiled up at me, so I continued. "Alessia and I were playing one night, and it went too far. She kept wanting more, pushing me to do things I wasn't comfortable with, and I should never have given in. Our dynamic differed from ours. When she asked for things, I gave them to her, but I never should have changed plans in the middle of a scene. She started bleeding a lot. More than I had ever seen. I begged her to let me get help, but she refused. She insisted she was fine, that it was normal, but then she started to shiver and her body felt cold. The blood never stopped, and she lost consciousness. I should have run to get someone. I should have done more, but I didn't. We were naked, covered in blood, and she was lying dead in my arms. Or so I thought. I ran. When I got to the house, Dante, Ares and I flew back to the States. I never heard her name mentioned again. I had assumed her family was trying to protect her reputation. No one would want it publicized that their daughter died by bleeding out in a sex scene."

"Nico, I... I don't know what to say."

"Mr. Corsetti met with me a few months later. He said he knew what happened and I wouldn't be allowed back to Sicily. He told me he could only protect me in New York and if I left, there was nothing he could do. So I never left, we never spoke of it. I tried to move on, but it ate at me every day that I had killed the woman I loved. It changed me as a person."

"But she didn't die."

"No, she didn't. You can imagine my surprise when I looked up to see her walking down the hallway at The Social. When I woke up and you were gone, I was enraged. I wanted nothing more than to destroy her for ruining me and coming for you. It wasn't until I had been at their villa for a few days that she told me what had happened. Massimo had seen me running from the house and went to check on her. He had assumed we broke up, but instead he found his sister bleeding out. If he hadn't been there, she would have died."

"Holy hell."

"Yeah."

"Are you mad at me for offering to help her?"

"No. I loved her at one point, Valentina. I can't pretend that I didn't. But I love you now, and I always will."

"You do?"

I smiled down at her and pulled her to me. "I love you more than anything in this world. I didn't think I could love again, but you constantly prove me wrong about myself."

My lips met hers. The fire between us ignited, and I pushed her back onto the bed and covered her body with mine. Her little whimpers of need as her legs wrapped around me were the only reassurance I needed. Valentina was my world, and I could only pray I was hers.

"Do you forgive me for what I said?"

"Maybe."

I thrust my hard cock into her center. "How about now?"

"Take your clothes off and let's see if you can make it up to me." she said with a wink.

I stood and stripped out of everything I had just put on, as Valentina pulled her clothes off in record time.

"Fuck, I've missed you," I growled as I barreled toward her, biting down on the side of her breast as soon as I got close enough.

"Wait!"

I froze mid movement.

"What's wrong?"

"Did you... did you sleep with her? While you were gone, I mean... if you did, it's okay. I just want to know."

I looked down and saw the tears pooling in her eyes. "No, my sweet girl. I didn't even so much as kiss her."

Valentina let out a huge breath and then laughed. "Good, because I know I said it was okay, but I don't think I really believed it would be."

"I always knew I was coming back to you. You're my world. I'd never do anything to hurt you like that."

I leaned over and placed a soft kiss on her lips. Trying to slow things down for her benefit, not mine, but Valentina had different plans. Her hand ran through my hair, and she held me to her. It has been far too long.

"Please, Nico. I need you."

"La mia bella ragazza, I'm going to fuck you so hard, they will hear you screaming my name on the other side of the house."

I shifted my hips and lined myself up with her entrance. In one long slow thrust, I entered her and pushed forward until I heard that sweet gasp of pleasure escape her lips. There was no stopping things. She had wrapped her legs around me and lifted her hips, allowing me even deeper than before. I continued to fuck her as she begged for more, even though I knew I wouldn't last. I rolled us over so she was on top of me and pulled her down until I could suck on her taut nipples. She loved it when I had them in my mouth, and from the way her hips ground into me, I could tell she was close. I slipped a finger between us and gently stroked her clit. Once, twice, three times was all she needed before she screamed out her release and her body tensed over mine. The feel of her clenching around my cock pulled my climax from me and I let go for the first time in weeks while she shouted my name for everyone to hear.

CHAPTER NINE

DANTE

"It sounds like Nico and our little girl made up," Ares said with a ridiculous grin on his face.

"Did you think it would take them long?"

"Not at all. In fact, I'm surprised he didn't pull the car over on the way here to fuck her until she forgave him."

"I'm not sure that would have worked. We saw a whole new side of Valentina today, one we shouldn't underestimate."

"Do you think she would have really killed Alessia?"

"I do."

"Are you going to let that go?"

It was a good question; one I had been thinking about all afternoon. Part of Valentina learning her place included her need to play politics with our family and others. The Corsetti Family spent years, even before my time, forging relationships with so many others. I can't have her just popping off whenever her feelings are hurt. Today was different, though. Her love for Nico was deep. I saw it the day we brought her back here without him, and every day after that. Our little girl loves fiercely and I can't fault her for that. If she had killed Alessia, we would have had a full-fledged war on our hands, a war I was negotiating daily to avoid.

"For now, I think I am. She has a lot to learn, but I don't know if this is the best example. Her love for Nico made her irrational. It's hard to teach her a lesson about something that I would do if the roles were reversed."

"You'd kill Alessia for Valentina?"

"I'd kill anyone for her. Wouldn't you?"

"I would."

"She will get punished for inviting her into our home, though. Those are decisions she can't make on her own. They need to be made between all of us. I could tell by the look on her face she knew that when she made the offer. Which means she intentionally displeased me."

"I figured as much," Ares said with a small laugh, "Are we leaving them alone tonight or do you want to speak with her?"

"Let's give them some time. We need to make arrangements with the other families for when we arrive in New York. We'll get everything settled tonight, so tomorrow we can have a day together. I'd like to fly out Friday morning. The club is fine, but we were supposed to close on two pieces of real estate last week and I needed to put them both off."

"Yeah, I know, Christy Calvano called me twice asking what our plans were."

"I appreciate she handles our real estate, even though she's with her husband's firm now. I'd rather not piss her off. She's the best one out there."

"Sofia called too. She said she had been trying to reach you, but you weren't answering, and she got nervous."

Sofia Corsetti was a cousin I recently found after going through some of my father's journals. Turns out my cousin's father had an affair with her mother when we were all children. She'd had a rough time adjusting to our family, but since she met her fiancé, things have been easier for her to deal with. I can understand that now more than I could before. With Valentina around, things just seemed easier. I don't know how to explain it really, it's just that everything else around us seems minor to her happiness and safety.

"I'll call her tonight. Can you call Anton and ask him to reach out to the other families? I want an in-person invitation for each of them, not phone calls."

"Sure, no problem."

"Thanks, I'm going to grab a shower and then fix something to eat. Nico and Valentina may be busy fucking, but they will need to come up for air eventually. When was the last time she ate?"

"She only had breakfast. By lunchtime she had worked herself up into a tizzy, insisting I bring her to Nico before we leave."

"I'll bring her something now, then."

I got up and headed into the kitchen. We had staff that maintained the property while we were away and the same people would take care of us while we were here, but with Valentina so upset I had wanted some privacy. The elderly couple that ran everything had a smaller house on the back of our property, so they were close in case anything came up, but otherwise we did fine on our own. I opened the fridge and found a bunch of prepared meals. Maria, Rodulfo's wife, was our cook, and no matter how many times I told her not to go to too much trouble, she never listened. I pulled out meatballs and a lasagna to warm up for dinner, then reached for a couple of bottles of water and some fruit.

Once I made my way down the hall to Nico's room, I heard them talking instead of fucking, so I knocked. Seeing Valentina with a smile on her face again moved something deep inside of me. I was fighting a losing battle as I tried not to fall in love with her.

"I brought food and water."

"Did you not eat?" Nico asked, turning to Valentina, who just looked the other way.

"She's not been eating well, or sleeping."

"Little girl, look at me. That is not okay."

"I know. I'm sorry," she said, looking at Nico, then back up at me. "I didn't mean to become such a problem."

"You're not a problem Ragazzina, you could never be a problem."

"Dante is right, but one of the very first things we discussed was how it was important to take care of yourself."

"I've gotten better. I've been eating for Ares."

"Only because he persuaded her with his cock," I said, raising an eyebrow in her direction.

"Is nothing a secret around here?"

"No," Nico and I both said in unison.

"Not when it comes to you." I handed her a pear. "Now eat this. I'm warming up dinner."

"You're warming up dinner?" she asked with a smile.

"Yes, I can warm up food. I'm not completely useless."

Her laugh made me want to pull her from Nico's bed and take her for myself, but I just enjoyed her happiness that had been missing for too many days.

"Do you guys think I could cook a few nights a week? I miss working in the kitchen."

When I thought back to our time in New York, we hadn't really offered Valentina much of anything to do. It was only a few weeks, but we spent most of that time bonding and fucking. Not that it was a bad thing, however, she needed to pursue things she enjoyed as well.

"Yes, of course. I would love for you to cook for us. It's time we figure out what our future will look like long term. I'm sure there is more you want out of life than just lying around and waiting to be fucked," I said with a wink.

"Fucked? Who said fucked? Am I being left out of our first foursome?" Ares asked as he came up behind me.

"No, you aren't, and it won't be tonight either," Nico said, giving the both of us a look to get lost.

"Fine, I get it. We already figured you guys would need some time alone tonight."

"Thank you," Valentina said, reaching for Nico's hand.

"Now get out," he added.

"I'll call you guys when dinner is done."

I turned around and pushed Ares out of the room in front of me as the sound of Valentina's laughs and giggles traveled throughout the room.

"What are we going to do about Angelo and his son?"

When dinner was done, Nico and Valentina found their way back to his bedroom, and Ares and I were sitting outside. I loved the mild weather and sound of the ocean. This was one of my favorite times of year to be in Sicily and I made a note to spend more time here in the coming months.

"I think there is only one thing we can do."

"Kill them?"

"Not both of them. When I called in Calvano Security to handle the auction, it brought a legal implication that we can't avoid. If we kill Angelo now, we will have a mess of time dodging the cops."

"Can't we just pay them off? Or hire someone else?"

"The thought has certainly crossed my mind. I think the bigger problem we have is Valentina's cousin Mario. We should have never let him that close to her."

"We won't do that again."

"No, no, we won't. When we get back, I'll send some guys for Angelo's son. He's an addict. It will be easy to make it look like an overdose. If Angelo doesn't take that as a warning and continues to cause problems, then we will deal with him. But for now, let's leave him to the FBI."

"And Mario?"

This situation with Mario was something I was going to need to discuss with Valentina. As much as I just wanted to move forward and make decisions to protect our family, he was her cousin and one of her only living blood relatives. After what he had put her through, I doubted she would be quick to forgive him, but that also didn't mean she wanted him dead.

"I don't know yet. Did you call your psychologist friend?"

"Yeah, he's willing to come here, but would prefer to stay in New York. I called Massimo just before dinner and he's going to talk to Alessia tonight. If she stays with us while she is being treated, it may be easier for everyone."

"Yeah, but then she's still in our house."

"It will be fine. Besides, if she acts up, we'll just have Valentina threaten her again."

"Not funny."

"Actually, it is. I want to take her shooting when we get home. See what she's really got in her."

"The tattoo parlor, now to the range? Ares, you aren't going to just take her all over New York parading her around on dates."

"Why not? She deserves all of that from us. Stop letting your fear of losing her drive all of your decisions."

"I'm not fucking scared of losing her."

"Sure. Keep telling yourself that."

"Fuck off."

"All I'm saying is you were an even bigger pain in the ass when she was gone. If she didn't matter that much to you, then why did you even care she was gone?"

"I didn't say she doesn't mean something to me. What I said was I wasn't scared."

He stood and looked down at me while I took a sip of my scotch, "You are scared because you love her and the sooner you admit it to yourself, the easier this will be for all of us."

I watched as Ares turned and went back into the house. His words pissed me off. There was nothing wrong with having a marriage based on friendship and physical attraction. If I tried to be something I wasn't, then I could fuck things up for all of us. We had so many issues to deal with right now. The last thing I needed was judgement from Ares. Besides, I wasn't making decisions based on fear. I was making them based on the same things I always had. What would benefit us most as a family.

CHAPTER TEN

VALENTINA

Flying on a private jet will be one of those things that I'll never get used to. As soon as we landed, there was a car waiting to take us to the house. It had been so long since I was home a feeling of nostalgia came over me as we drove onto the property. The Corsetti Estate felt more like a home to me than my father's house ever felt. The only problem I was facing now was that as soon as we walked in, everyone moved in opposite directions. Dante was already on the phone yelling at someone while Ares wasn't far behind him, heading into the office. I knew they would be busy, but even Nico gave me a quick kiss, then disappeared to a building he had on the border of the woods that he called his workshop. It was one of many places I hadn't ventured to yet, and I wasn't thinking it was something I'd do anytime soon. Ares' comments about it made me wonder what Nico actually worked on in there, and that wasn't something I wanted an answer for yet.

I unpacked, cleaned up, and changed my clothes. I walked around my room, the place Ares had created for me before he had even known me, and smiled. The books on the shelves and the artwork on the walls screamed his style, and I loved everything about it. Then there were little things that I knew had been left behind by the others. Late one night, I was opening drawers in my closet and found a velvet lined drawer full of knives. I hadn't remembered it being there before, but I didn't do a thorough investigation of everything either. I knew they were from Nico as soon as I saw them. They were beautiful and engraved with "La mia bella ragazza."

In the drawer above them was Dante's gift. The drawer was empty, but inside of it was a box. Inside was a diamond encrusted collar. Each of them had provided me with things that meant something to them, but Dante's gift was the one that made me gasp. I knew exactly what it was and why he had given it to me, but it still wasn't time for me to wear it. Every night when I went to my closet to change for bed, I would open the box and run my fingers over the cool stones. Someday I would feel confident enough in my relationship with him to wear it, but today still wasn't that day.

I put everything away and headed down to the kitchen. My constant craving for some chocolate chip cookies was something I was looking forward to fulfilling, but I knocked before barging in.

"Hi."

"Ms. Romano, good to see you back. Is there something I can get for you?" Elizabeth was one of the girls who worked here and always so sweet. She looked to be about my age and had a kind smile to greet me with.

"I was hoping maybe I could bake some cookies."

"Oh, you don't have to do that. I'll prepare them for you. What would you like?"

"Umm... honestly, I was hoping to do it myself. I promise I'll keep out of your way, if you could just help me find a few things."

"Are you sure?"

"Yes. Really, I used to love spending time in the kitchen at my father's and I really miss it."

"This is kind of embarrassing to ask, but I don't want to get into trouble... did you check with Mr. Corsetti?"

I smiled and reached for her hand. "Please don't ever be embarrassed to ask me anything. I would never want to get you or anyone else here in any kind of trouble. To answer your question, yes, I spoke with Dante and he's fine with me preparing some meals and working in here. I just wanted to make sure it's okay with you first."

"I mean, it's your kitchen as much as it's his, so of course you are welcome."

"Elizabeth, I think you know as well as I do Dante wouldn't know a colander from a cast iron pan. This is your kitchen, not his," I said with a laugh.

Her smile made me hopeful that maybe I could find a friend here after all. I loved Dante, Ares and Nico, but I never really had a friend before, at least not anyone I considered a friend. There were people in my family's circles that were friendly, but no one I could sit and spend time with.

"Come with me. I'll show you around."

Elizabeth showed me where to find just about anything I could think of in the kitchen and pantry. We shared lunch together and laughed over everything from Nico's grumpy moods to her best friend Dominic's crazy antics to get her attention. I loved every minute of it.

"So tell me, if you two grew up together and you get along so well, why in the world have you not agreed to date him?"

"We are too different. He's from a very wealthy family and I'm not. People from different backgrounds struggle to make things work."

"But it's just money."

"No, it's not. Dominic is an Italian with strong cultural beliefs, and I'm a black girl from South Carolina. My mom scraped by to pay for my culinary degree. This job has been a blessing because I can finally pay her back, but her expectation is I move home and marry a good black southern boy from church. Dominic's family only vacationed near my hometown. Their actual home is here in New York City. Once I pay my mom back, I'll leave and he'll stay here."

"But that's not fair. I mean, I get wanting to pay your mom back for your degree, but you don't owe her your whole life."

"Valentina, the people here don't operate like the rest of the world. Maybe if our worlds weren't so different, we would stand a chance, but I gave up that hope years ago. Now my prayers at night are that Dominic finds a good woman who won't mind that he has a crazy southern girl for a best friend, " she said with a wink.

"Am I interrupting anything?" Ares' voice carried through the kitchen, and the smile that came over my face was almost embarrassing. I turned to find him standing in the doorway, looking as gorgeous as ever.

"Come here. I want you to try something," I said, holding a cookie up for him to take a bite out of.

"Damn, that's delicious. What did you put in it?"

"It's a secret," I said as he pulled me to his body and invaded my space with everything that was Ares. I swooned and made the most ridiculous sound, then immediately cringed when I remembered we weren't alone.

"You two are so cute," Elizabeth said as I pushed Ares away and went to help her clean up the mess we had left.

"When you're done in here, we'd like to see you. Can you come to the office?"

"Yeah, no problem." Ares seemed off, almost serious rather than his usual playful self, which put me on edge.

"Go ahead, Valentina. I've got this."

"Are you sure?"

"Yes, of course. There isn't much left to do and I'm going to get started on dinner, anyway."

I pulled Elizabeth in for a quick hug. "Thank you so much for today. I had so much fun."

"Me too, and you are always welcome in here while I'm working."

I smiled, then reached for Ares' hand as we made our way back through the house.

"What's going on?"

"Nothing, why?"

"You seem off."

"I'm fine. How was your afternoon?"

"Wonderful. Like maybe one of the best days I've had in years."

He stopped and pulled me into his arms. "I love hearing that. I can't wait for every day to be better than the next."

I stood there for a minute and let him hold me. Something was definitely bothering him. Dante and Nico both joked that Ares was the bleeding heart of the bunch, but I think it had more to do with him being empathetic. He fed off other people's energy and when everyone was stressed, he would be too. Walking into the office didn't help any. Dante was sitting behind his desk with his eyes glued to his laptop, and Nico was propped up in the corner, staring out the window. What I hadn't expected was the third man who was sitting across from Dante. I hesitated going to Dante, but pushed through it. I knew having three men in my life was out of the norm, but I needed to get used to providing attention to them all, even with others around. They were my world and that was nothing to be ashamed of. I walked over to Dante first and leaned over to place a kiss on his cheek. He turned when he felt my lips on his skin and wrapped his hand in my hair. I gasped, which gave him the entrance he needed. His kiss was desperate and needy. We hadn't had enough time together lately, and I felt guilty about it. When he released me, I went to Nico, who pulled me to his body and kissed my neck. I could feel the cool metal of his knife press into my side and it sent a chill of desire to rush through my body. If this is what hello looked like, then I was in for a lifetime of happiness.

"Valentina, I want you to meet Anton Tirelli. When the three of us are tied up, he is the man who takes care of everything."

"It's nice to meet you, Anton."

"You as well. I've heard a lot about you over the years. I'm happy to see you are home."

My eyes drifted over to Dante, but his expression didn't let me in on a thing.

"I understand you met Alessia De Bartoli while in Sicily," Anton continued.

"You could say that," I said as I took a seat next across from Dante's desk.

"She's always been a little hot-tempered. I made it a rule years ago to not allow her and my wife in the same room. She and Maya would burn this place down with their drama."

"You could say that again," Nico added.

"Did you know she was alive?"

"No, I only found out when Dante did. However, Maya and I were friends and lovers long before we were married. Childhood sweethearts, I supposed you would call it."

"More like childhood torture," Ares added with a laugh, which Anton responded to by throwing a pen he was holding at his head.

Dante just shook his head and began to talk, "There are some plans we have been working on and in an effort of full disclosure, I wanted you to be aware of what's coming."

"Plans about what?"

"You, us, the situation we have found ourselves in. First, it's important for you to understand that when it comes to the business, you can speak freely in front of Anton. There are not many people we trust as much as him, but we have known him as long as we've known each other. His father was my father's right-hand man and although it took me years to convince Anton to work for me, now that he's here, I keep nothing from him."

"Okay."

"They have released Angelo Costa on bail, and since we did not report your kidnapping, they never went after Mateo for his involvement.

"I understand that."

"Angelo is set for trial, and we are going to leave him alone until then. Once he is found guilty and placed in prison, he won't have anyone to protect him. Angelo will die once he arrives there. As for Matteo, he's an addict. I believe that's something you were already aware of. Ares has located him and Nico will be... working on getting the truth from him."

I turned to Nico, who had a sick smile on his face. "Working how?"

"How do you think, my pretty girl?"

I sat there for a minute, looking at Nico and then the others. That's when I realized what was going on. I didn't know what to say, not because it bothered me. But because it didn't. If Nico tortured Matteo for the truth in the same way, the rumors said, he had others; I was okay with that, and I struggled with how it made me feel.

"Valentina, are you okay?" Ares' voice cut through the silence but I didn't answer him. I looked up at Nico, whose eyes hadn't left mine.

"I want to see."

"Okay," Nico said at the same time Dante said, "No."

"Why not?"

"Because I said so."

"No, it doesn't work that way. You don't get to just lay down the law and we all have to follow it. It's up to Nico, not you."

"Anything that has to do with your wellbeing has to do with me," Dante said as anger rose in his voice.

"My wellbeing isn't what is in question here. I want to see Nico work. If he doesn't have a problem with that, then you shouldn't either."

Dante's grip on the arms of his chair had tightened. I knew I was pushing it but I didn't care.

I glanced at Anton, who had a smirk on his face. "Maybe I should give you all a minute. Seems like Valentina isn't so different from my Maya, after all."

"No, stay," Dante ordered, then looked in my direction, "We will continue this conversation later."

I rolled my eyes at him, and he nearly came out of his chair. For some reason, pushing him was like a high today, even when Ares laughed at the disaster I was creating for myself. At least he had a smile on his face rather than the look of impending doom he had earlier.

"Valentina, watch yourself," Dante warned in a voice that made me wet. I shifted in my seat and he seemed pleased with my discomfort. "The bigger problem we have right now is your cousin. Before we left, we had a shipment that went missing. Anton determined Mario is the one to blame for it. A minor infraction compared to setting you up for Matteo, but still it's something you need to be aware of."

"What will happen to him?"

"I will kill him," Nico said, but Dante held his hand up before he could continue.

"He is your family. I want you to consider what you would like to happen. He can not stay in the city. He has become too much of a threat to you and our business. I can have him sent away or I can give him to Nico. But the choice will be yours."

"Did you ever find out why he helped Matteo?" I asked Nico.

"For money. The Costas accountant transferred him a large amount of money the day you were taken. Ares found it."

"Money. It always came down to money and power with my cousin."

"You can give some thought to what you want done, but we need to move quickly. Matteo was easy to pick up, but Mario has already been calling in favors with the other families. While we were gone, Anton met with them all to set up a meeting. There were quite a few who disclosed that he had been in touch."

"I want to talk to him."

"No." All three of my men responded that time.

"Not alone. You can be there. I want him to tell me to my face that he wanted to trade me to a psycho for money."

CHAPTER ELEVEN

DANTE

"Do you know why you're here?" I asked Valentina as she was bound and kneeling in front of me.

"Because I disrespected you, sir."

"I thought you had known us well enough by now. I thought you would have realized how important it is to ask before offering our home to someone. Was I ignorant, Ragazzina, or were you disobedient?"

She opened her mouth, then closed it. I could tell she was confused about her punishment and I wanted her to tell me why.

"I was disobedient, sir."

"Is there something you'd like to ask?"

She raised her head slightly and met my gaze. "I thought I'd be punished for taking Nico's gun."

"No. But you will need to learn a certain decorum when interacting with other families. We all understand you were upset over Nico's situation, so I will let that go. This time. But in the future, you can not just threaten whoever you'd like."

Nico let out a grunt from where he was watching. I'm sure he'd love to have our little girl running all over town fighting our battles with us, but there was no way I'd let that happen. Tonight was the first night she'd have us all, and she was already on edge. Her body was covered in goosebumps as I ran a riding crop across her shoulders.

"Tonight I will let you choose your punishment. Stand up."

Even with her arms bound behind her, she stood gracefully. I placed the crop down on the table I had set up and untied her hands. "Come with me."

She followed just a step behind me and her eyes went wide when she got a clear look at the table in front of her.

"These are the toys we have for you. Tonight, you will begin deciding parts of our scenes. We can set new perimeters every time or there can be certain things you can choose that you never want to do. One thing that will not be tolerated is adding anything new to a scene once we have already started." The way she looked up at me, absorbing every word I had to say, made her even more tempting. I pointed to the table and explained some of what was there. "Floggers vary in intensity. This one for instance, is made from a thick heavy rubber. The impact is very hard. It feels more like a thud than a sting. This is a snake whip, it stings. Much like this cane, or even my riding crop."

"What's that?"

"It's called a Dragon's Tail. It's loud but doesn't hurt much. The noisier the toy, the less the impact. It's the quiet ones that are more intense."

Valentina ran her hand over each of them, inspecting and considering what I had shared. She picked up a leather flogger and ran it over her palm, smiling at the sensation. Then she moved on to the cane. It was a bamboo cane with a black handle. She turned it in her hand a few times before looking back at me.

"I would be fine with any of these. There are none I want to remove."

"You're certain?"

"I am."

"Very well then. Go to Ares. He will place you."

Valentina moved to the bed where Ares had sat, leaned up against the headboard. He pulled her onto his lap and over his already hard cock. She leaned forward to kiss him as he lined himself up with her center. I reached for my first toy of choice just as I heard her gasp.

"Don't move now," he said, "You are only here to receive your punishments."

The pout she gave him was so fucking cute I wanted to devour her. She knew what was coming, but our greedy little doll wanted more than she was going to get at that moment. Ares pulled her to his chest and made her lay flat against him. Her ass stuck up perfectly as he caressed her back and placed kisses on the top of her head. I walked over to them and watched as she slowly closed her eyes and relaxed. Just as her breathing evened out, I reached back and swung the snake whip forward, making perfect contact with her plump little ass. She screamed out and her body tensed, causing Ares to curse and hold her tight.

"One."

"Damn, that left a pretty mark," Nico said from behind me.

Again.

"Two."

The split tongue of the whip left gorgeous red marks on her backside that I wanted to suck into my mouth.

"Three. Four," I continued as she whimpered and tears came to her eyes.

"Tell me again Ragazzina, why are you being punished?"

"For inviting someone into our home."

"Five. Six," I continued, "And will you do that again?"

"No, sir. Never."

"Seven. Eight."

By the eighth strike, she was red all over. I picked up the soft leather flogger and ran it gently over her irritated skin. She shivered under the feel of it, and I watched as she rocked her hips forward slightly.

"You do not have permission to come, little girl."

She froze over Ares, who looked as if he was receiving his own punishment. He had asked specifically to be holding her while she got spanked tonight. His choice in the way he held her was completely his own. I took the flogger and ran through a quick succession of hits. Covering her already swelling ass with a whole unique feeling.

"She's so wet," Ares said, "I can feel her juices dripping down my balls."

Nico knelt next to her on the bed as he palmed his dick. She pushed herself up from Ares and looked hungrily in his direction. “Is my little slut making a mess of her man’s cock?”

“Mmmmhmmmm,” she moaned and then licked her lips.

“Such a little whore. That greedy cunt of yours is going to get you in trouble tonight.”

She turned back to me, “I’m sorry sir, I promise I didn’t come.”

I nodded my head in Nico’s direction. He reached for the back of her neck and turned her to him. In one smooth movement, she opened her mouth in surprise, only to find it filled with his cock.

“Maybe that will distract you,” I said, as I reached for the lube. I put the toys back on the table. I would have loved to continue, but none of us were going to last much longer. Valentina with Ares’ cock in her pussy and Nico’s in her mouth was just too much. I needed to be inside of her now. I coated myself in lube and got on the bed between Ares’ legs. Valentina was sucking on Nico as if he was the best thing she had tasted all day. He had a hold of her head and controlled the pace as Ares pinched her nipples and rolled them between his fingers. I placed my hand on her hip and dipped a finger inside her tight rosebud, coating it with more lube, before I lined myself up and pushed my way into her. She was so fucking tight I had to bite my lip to keep from crying out. I hadn’t taken time to prepare her, but we had been slowly working our way up in size with her plugs. She could take me. I knew she could and so did she. Her body tensed and she stilled for only a second and then continued on Nico’s cock.

I worked with Ares, moving her forward and backward as she moaned out at the fullness of it all.

"That's a good girl. You're such a good girl," I said as I pressed harder into her than before. Valentina was perfection. I looked over into the mirror and admired her as I fucked her ass. Her hair was falling out of the braid I put it in and all bunched up in Nico's hand. Her eye makeup was running down her face with tears and her chin was covered in spit. I looked down at where my body entered hers and couldn't draw my eyes away. Her moans and whimpers were turning into cries and I knew we didn't have much time left.

"Not yet, Ragazzina."

Nico pulled out of her mouth and leaned over to kiss her. It was forceful, and she reached for him, pulling him closer to her. I nodded at Ares, who slipped his finger in between them. I felt her body tense as soon as he stroked her clit.

"I can't... please... I need to..." she was muttering nonsense. I knew what she needed. We all needed it. Nico leaned back on his heels and continued to jerk his cock as he watched. Valentina was in full on hysterics trying to hold back her climax as I felt the first sign I was losing control.

"Now, give it to us now."

She screamed out her release with a noise so violent I would have thought Nico had stabbed her. My orgasm hit at the same time while her body clenched onto my cock, I emptied myself into her sweet little ass. Ares wasn't far behind me. I pulled out from her slowly and he gripped her hips, rocking her weak body over him and taking what he needed until he was spent. I stood to clean up as Nico pulled Valentina from Ares' arms. He laid her onto the bed and held her legs up in front of him, placing one on either shoulder as he plunged inside her and growled his pleasure when her body took him in.

"That's my good little slut. Do you like that? Filled with their cum and still needing more."

Valentina went from laying there in a daze to taking him in fully as he degraded her and punished her with his cock. I knew I should walk away, go get a towel and start a bath, but the look on her face mesmerized me. He pounded into her so hard she screamed every time. Her hands gripped the sheets and her head writhed back-and-forth as she screamed out his name. There was no way she had even come down completely from her last high and her body was already climbing to new levels. He let her legs fall to the side, and she wrapped them around him. I went to her and reached for her neck, holding her down to the bed as she cried out.

"Please, sir," she begged me again. She was ready, but it just wasn't the time yet. I smiled as I shook my head no and then Ares' hand appeared between us with a little black wand. Her eyes went wide and Nico leaned back, making just enough room for Ares to reach her clit with it. Her screams were deafening. Nico continued to fuck her as I leaned over to quiet her mouth with my own. Ares smiled as the small vibrating torture device had her biting her lip so hard it bled.

"That's mine," Nico grunted and nodded his head toward the blood.

I moved my hand from her neck and grasped her breast in one hand while slapping her nipple hard with my other.

"Do you want to come, Ragazzina?"

"Yes, please."

"Is it time for your little slut, Nico?"

"Yes, it's time."

"Go." One word of instruction was all she needed. Even with the three of us holding her down, her hips thrust forward and her body shook beneath us as pure pleasure crossed her face. Nico grunted his release, and when Ares moved back, he leaned forward, licking the blood from her lips.

"La mia bella ragazza, how will we ever get enough of you?"

I placed a kiss on her forehead, then stood and made my way to the bathroom. I ran a bath for Valentina and started the shower for myself. After a few minutes, Nico came in with her, carrying her into the oversized tub with Ares not far behind. I watched as they cared for her, washed her and kissed her. She moaned when Ares took her nipples into his mouth and Nico's fingers slid beneath the water. He was right about one thing, we would never get enough of her. I dried off and pulled out the ointments we would need to tend to her wounds. More than one strike had broken skin and her lip would be sore in the morning. As they got her out and dried her off, I went to the kitchen. With water, snacks, and an ice pack in hand, I made my way back to them. Tonight would be a night we'd all stay together. Too much had passed between us for us to separate, and I was fine with that. Valentina was lying naked on my bed with her red little ass, just waiting for care. I had never seen anything more beautiful than that.

CHAPTER TWELVE

ARES

I had a feeling this was a bad idea from the beginning, but Nico insisted Valentina needed to see everything, feel everything, and be part of everything. She never gave us a solid answer about what she wanted us to do with Mario, and Dante wasn't pressing her on it. But this was different. Nico and I pulled up to the underpass that housed most of the addicts from this side of town. I had received word about an hour earlier that Mateo was spotted here. It was time to end one of our problems. Nico was out of the SUV before I even pulled it to a full stop. I got out as he was shouting into the crowd of people, waving his knives around like some crazy idiot. I shook my head as I pulled my gun out and removed the safety. He had been relatively calm since our return from Sicily, but I knew that was Valentina's influence. As we worked together throughout the day, he would grow increasingly agitated until he got back to her. I don't think either of them realized how addicted they had grown to each other. It was after nine at night and we were busy making rounds all day. He called Dante a ridiculous amount of times to speak with her, which just pissed Dante off. I got a text message from him about an hour ago telling me to get her a phone or he would stop answering the phone when Nico called. "Alright you fuckers! Where is he?" Nico shouted as he moved through a group of people who seemed completely unamused by his insanity act. I'm certain they've seen worse, and I know they've seen Nico like this before.

"Who you here for this time, Marchesi?" One of the larger guys shouted.

"Mateo Costa."

That brought more eyes in our direction than before. Everyone was quiet, but the man who spoke up originally pointed in the direction we were headed.

Nico slipped his hand in his pocket and gave the guy a hundred-dollar bill. "Don't kill yourself tonight."

The man shook his head in agreement, pocketed the money and ran in the direction we were headed. Likely to whatever dealer was there for the night. Drugs were a messy business and although it was a business we were in, we handled things much higher up the food chain. Our product was clean and expensive. Rarely did it make it to the streets, but instead to the assholes on Wall Street and the shitty politicians who hid their coke habits from not only their wives but also their mistresses.

I followed Nico back into the dark covered area where clusters of users sat around each other, either tweaking for their next high or practically unconscious from their last one. That's how we found Mateo. He stood out like a sore thumb. He was dressed in a three-piece suit with his tie and a top few buttons undone. His right foot was missing a sock and shoe and he was braced up against a pile of cardboard boxes with a needle sitting next to him. It didn't take a genius to figure out what he had been up to.

Nico reached down and pulled his dazed body up by his shirt. "Time's up, motherfucker."

Mateo couldn't even speak. His head rolled to the side, and he laughed. Nico dropped him back into the heap he was in, then bent and lifted him over his shoulder. I let him walk ahead of me as we made it back to the car. There were some perks to being The Dark Kings and a night like this was one of them. People were ready and willing to provide us with information. They knew we'd pay. They also never fucked with our cars, which made me smile as we walked by someone who was holding a metal shim next to the driver's window of a car parked near ours. When we got to the SUV, I opened the door and Nico dumped Mateo into the back. Just for good measure, I reached in and tied his wrists together with some zip ties, but he was so fucked up it was impossible to tell if he even knew what was happening.

Two hours later, we had strung Mateo up in Nico's workshop, and he and Dante were still arguing over Valentina.

"You will not involve her in this shit."

"Why? Because you said so? Not a good enough reason. He was the one who thought he could get to her. I'm going to kill him and she's going to watch."

"Absolutely not."

I shook my head at the two of them. Valentina was already annoyed with all of us since we sent her off to bed alone. The entire argument was pointless because Nico was going to do whatever he wanted to do. Dante wasn't an idiot, but sometimes when he'd argue with Nico like this, I questioned his sanity. The more you told Nico no, the more motivated he was to do it. I was done with the bullshit.

"I'm going to bed. You two can argue all you want, but I'd rather be dick deep in my doll."

They both shot me an evil look, but I didn't care. When I got to the other side of the house, I found Valentina in her own room. We let her choose where she wanted to sleep every night. None of us had any qualms about climbing into whatever bed she was in, but it was clear she wasn't pleased with any of us since she hadn't picked one of our rooms.

"Baby doll. Can I come in?"

She rolled over and faced the wall but didn't tell me no, so I went to her. I lifted the blanket covering her small body and pulled her to me. "Do you want to talk about it?"

"No."

"Okay. Can I hold you or do you want me to go?"

"You can stay."

I nuzzled my nose into her neck and reveled in her smell. I swear, if those two assholes would just get up here in bed, then everything would be forgotten. Valentina had this effect on all of us. I'd lay in bed some days and dream of the day we retire from this life. A life with just us and her and none of the shit. It seemed like a pipe dream most days, but I still pretended in the depths of my mind that it would be a possibility.

“I don’t like it when they argue about me.”

I smiled to myself. She needed to talk, after all. “I know you don’t.”

“Dante acts like Nico is an idiot and incapable of making decisions for me. And Nico makes decisions for me without even asking me what I want. I can decide for myself.”

“We know you can, and we all know that when you allow us to decide things for you it’s a choice you are making. But sometimes the situation is more complicated than what you may be used to.”

“You’re talking about Mateo.”

“What do you know about it?”

“I overheard one of the guards say you two were back. I got excited and ran out to see you, but you had already come inside. Instead, I saw some guys pulling him from the back of your SUV. He’s here, isn’t he?”

Our tricky little girl was at it again.

“You didn’t think that information was worth sharing with us?”

“Not when Dante thinks I’m some idiot who will crumble if I watch Nico kill him.”

“Little doll, how much do you know about what’s going on?”

“I might have been listening from the sitting room. Nico’s loud.”

I laughed. “You are incorrigible sometimes. Here we are, three grown men arguing over what’s best for you while trying to keep things from you. Yet you already know everything, don't you?"

"Maybe."

"Do you want to be with Nico when he deals with Mateo?"

"Yes."

"Alright, come on then. Let's go," I said, letting her go and pulling back the covers as I got out of bed.

"Where are we going?"

"To tell Dante and Nico they are idiots."

I walked toward the door as she ran up behind me and reached for my hand. I looked down at her and smirked. Not only was she about to put them in their place, but she was dressed in nearly nothing. Her nipples shone through the black lace nightie she had on and the black thong she wore under it left her ass free for me to grab... and I did. She smiled up at me with an excitement in her eyes that was more than just sex. We rounded the corner for the office and I pushed the double doors open. Nico and Dante immediately quieted and looked up at her. A smile came over Nico's face, but Dante kept his look of steel.

"Valentina has something she'd like to share with you both."

Nico squinted as Dante's eyebrows rose. Their expressions were never the same, but in this moment, the confusion was clear.

"Go on," I said, letting go of her hand and placing my hand on her back.

"I... I want to be with Nico when he kills Mateo."

"Ares, you are a fucking dick," Dante said before she had even finished her sentence.

"This wasn't me."

"It wasn't. I saw the guys pulling him from Ares' car when they got back, so I knew he was here."

Dante shot me another dirty look, as if I could have helped her from seeing it.

"Tell them everything, La mia piccola bambola."

"And I heard you arguing." She lowered her head for only a second but then she looked straight at the two of them. "I don't like you making decisions for me. Either of you. You promised to keep me in the loop about things, but every time I turn around, there are more secrets. I want to choose what I'm involved in, and I can't do that unless you tell me what's happening."

She took a step towards them and I let my hand drop. My little doll had gained the confidence she needed for this fight. With one hand on her hip, she pointed right at Nico. "Just because I want to be with you doesn't mean you won this fight. You should have asked me first instead of deciding it would be what I was going to do. And you..." she said as she turned back to Dante, "I am a fully grown woman. I let you decide things for me because I like it. But when you take away all of my choices, it pisses me off. Now, both of you finish up in here and come to bed. It's been a long day and tomorrow won't be much better."

She turned on her heel and gave me a little wink as she walked past. I laughed, and that only seemed to irritate the two brutes. "You heard the girl. Finish up in here. She has requested us in her bedroom."

"Fuck off," Nico threw as an insult, but I could hear him walking behind me. There was no way he would deny Valentina. It would take Dante a few minutes to regulate, and that was fine. I'm sure Nico and I could keep her busy until he got there.

CHAPTER THIRTEEN

VALENTINA

The house was rather somber the next morning. Dante, Nico, and Ares all slept in my room last night. Even with them all there, I didn't sleep well. I had dreams of chaos and nightmares of losing them all. Ares was the only one who questioned my quiet state, but I didn't want to get into it. I knew it was all because of what we had to do today. Nico got up earlier than usual and, after bringing me breakfast, went down to his workshop. He still hadn't come up to the main house, which made me wonder how today was going to go. I didn't think killing people was a big deal to any of them, especially if they were a threat to the family, but the reserved moods everyone was in had me on edge.

"Is it because I'm here?" I finally asked Ares as he watched me get dressed.

"Yes."

That he knew exactly what I was talking about without needing clarification only solidified the truth deep inside of me. I pulled on a pair of black chucks, black jeans and a black t-shirt. I looked like I was heading out for a rock concert, but the truth was, I didn't want to see the blood splatter. The night they came for me, I was covered in blood. For that reason alone, I'll never wear a white nightie again.

"Let's go then."

Ares stood and followed me out. We passed Dante in the hallway, and Ares nodded in his direction. I went out through the oversized glass doors that opened to the courtyard in the back of the house. I loved everything about the gardens and had just recently spent time working out there. Dante told me most of it was planted by his grandmother and he did everything he could to preserve the plants she loved in her memory. I figured helping the gardeners keep them well taken care of was the least I could do. When I reached the edge of the manicured lawn, I stepped into the shade of the forest behind our house. I had never come this far out before. I didn't need to be anywhere near this place. But now, looking at the little concrete building on the edge of the tree line, I realized it wasn't as frightening as I had imagined it.

"Ragazzina, this place is Nico's domain. We allow him to do whatever he needs while in here and try not to interrupt," Dante said as we approached.

"Okay."

"I don't know what his plans are for Mateo. He never shares and we never ask. I leave this part of our business to him. Do you understand what I'm saying?"

"Yes, I do."

"If anything you see in here upsets you, I want you to tell Ares or I and we will leave with you immediately."

"Nico doesn't scare me."

"I didn't say that he does."

"No, but you implied it. Which is insane because I thought we were past this." I took a step back and looked at both of them. "I know you are concerned about me, and I won't try to tell you not to be but if you both continue to question Nico's stability then we are going to have much bigger problems than trying to decide who sleeps next to who."

They both stood there in silence. Ares was looking at the ground as if it were the most interesting thing he'd ever seen and Dante was staring me down. At least they had the decency not to argue.

"Now, I'm going in there because I'm choosing to go. If there is something I don't want to see, I will leave, but otherwise, I'm staying with Nico. Got it?"

"Yes, little girl. I've...'Got it'" Dante said with more attitude than was necessary, and Ares just mumbled something incoherent. I turned and reached for the door. The smell of everything that had happened in there hit me like a wall of fury. There were faint smells of bleach which led me to believe it was cleaned at one point, but the stench of a dying man overpowered the smell of the strong chemical. Nico looked up when the bright light lit his workspace. He was standing behind a table, laying out what I could only explain as a small arsenal of weapons.

"La mia bella ragazza, you're here," he said with a soft smile that didn't fit our current situation. The large metal door we came through closed with a thud and made me jump. Nico frowned and came to me, pulling me in his arms.

"You are sure about this?"

"Yes, I am sure."

Nico's lips crashed into mine as he pulled my body closer to his. I moaned as he grabbed my ass and squeezed so tight that the sweet pain I loved ran through me.

"I have a surprise for you when we are done."

"What kind of surprise?" I whispered.

"Let's just say I'm happy you wore your sneakers." He winked and stepped back. "Come, let me show you my work."

Nico led me to the man that was hanging from large metal chains in the middle of the room. Mateo was wrecked, but most of it was because he was clearly going through withdrawal. A slick coating of sweat was running over his yellowed skin, yet he was shaking as if he were cold. His eyes were darting all over the room and I could see him switching neurotically from clenching his teeth to licking his lips. When I walked past him, his body lunged for me with no success. The movement made me jump, but there was no way he could get close. Nico stood between us and then just laughed when Mateo whined.

"Come on, man, just a hit. Give me a little something to take the edge off."

"He's been begging for drugs since I got down here. Interesting that he isn't begging for his life, or even to be let go."

I nodded my head slowly. Mateo was someone I had known for most of my life. He was older than me when we were kids and I never liked being around him. In his twenties, he earned the title of the devil and loved it. His sketchy and unpredictable behaviors only increased when he started using.

"Valentina, you can sit here or with Dante and Ares. It's up to you," Nico said, pointing to a folding chair he had set up.

"I want to stand with you, not sit in a corner."

He smiled down at me. "Of course, my little queen."

I watched as Nico made his way over to the table. He picked up his knife that he always played with and made his way back to me. He held it out. "Would you like to do the honors?"

Would I? It wouldn't have been the first time I pierced skin with a knife, but it wasn't mine. I reached for the blade and smirked as its heavy weight felt comforting in my hand.

"What do you plan to do with him?" I asked.

"Originally, I was going to just overdose him with his own shit and leave him on the streets to be found. But he's been singing like a canary since he woke up and a message needs to be sent."

"What did he say?"

"Our boy here is a liar. Although I could have figured that from the beginning. He had claimed full credit for taking you, but it wasn't you, was it, Mateo?"

"I already told you, that bitch offered me more money than I would have made selling her back to my father."

"See?"

"So many words for someone so desperate."

"The problem is, he didn't start with that story. We knew Alessia's involvement, but Mateo still wanted me to believe he hired her. You didn't do that, did you, Mateo?"

"No."

"Why not?"

"Because you froze all our fucking assets!" he screamed at Ares this time, who only laughed.

"But there is a bigger problem, isn't there?"

I watched as Nico got right up into Mateo's face, holding a blade of his own under the man's chin.

"Yes."

"Tell my little Queen what that problem is."

"Your cousin. He's trying to take over. He's gotten a few families to agree, but we didn't."

"Why not?"

"Because he didn't have enough money to pay us. Then he said he could get to you, so my father told him he'd have our support."

"Where is Mario now?"

"I don't know." Nico pressed the knife into the man's neck until a trickle of blood dripped. "Try again Mateo."

"I don't know, really I don't. When you picked me up, I had been down there for a few days. The last time I saw Mario was when you were still in Sicily. He held a meeting with the families and I went in my father's place."

I looked back at Dante with concern that this was new information. If it was, then he didn't let on this was the first time he had heard it. I looked back at Nico. "Hold him for me."

Nico straightened and looked back at me. "How would you like him?"

"I want access to his chest. But don't let him touch me."

"Of course." Nico bowed his head slightly and a mannerism I never would have expected. He slid his knife into his belt and stepped behind Mateo, holding his filthy body still while I approached.

I was so sick of these fucking men and their games. Mario had no right trying to work with anyone in power. He had to have been using my dead father's influence to rise up, and that was just total shit. Nico wanted to send a message. I get that. But this time, the message would be mine.

"Hold him still." As I raised my hand, I let the knife slice into his skin. He cried out in pain, which I ignored and Nico held him still as could be. I grinned as I carved my message into the body of a man who planned to sell me off to the highest bidder just to support his drug habit. I finished and took a step back, smiling at Nico over Mateo's shoulder. I had never seen such joy on his face. The crazed, manic Nico that I had seen in the video from my house wasn't the man I was staring at. The man I was looking at now loved me, and I loved him. For once in his life, he didn't feel like an outsider, and I'd do anything in my power to keep it that way. I reached my hand out for him and stepped aside so Dante and Ares could see what I did.

"Don't fuck with The Dark Queen," Ares read aloud, "Very nice, my little doll."

Nico leaned in and kissed my cheek while Dante allowed a rare smile to come over his face.

"I don't care what you do to him now. I've seen all I wanted."

Nico reached for his knife and took it from me, placed it back on the table, and picked up a gun. The shot was loud but efficient. Mateo didn't even see it coming. The pain from the words I carved into his skin distracted him. One bullet, almost perfectly centered in his forehead. Nico put the gun down and reached for my hand.

"Come with me."

"But... what about—"

"I'll clean up later. I want to show you something." He pulled me past Ares and Dante, who simply let us go. When we got outside, Nico broke out into a run but never let go of my hand. He was fast, and it was hard to keep up with him. The pace was punishing, but the burn in my chest reminded me I was alive. We ran through the brush and I felt the stinging scratch of a branch that had caught my arm. After a few minutes, we came to a clearing. Nico let go of my hand and stopped. I turned in circles as I caught my breath. Trees that felt larger than life surrounded us. The opening they created in the sky let the sun shine down onto us and the grass beneath our feet.

"What is this place?"

"It's my quiet place. Well, it was. Now my quiet place is with you."

"What do you mean?"

"Before we found you, the only time I could quiet my mind was when I laid here. Now I don't have to come here anymore, instead I just need to find you."

Tears sprung to my eyes before I could stop them. I didn't know if they were tears of happiness for what we had found or if I was grieving for the man who lived a tortured life for so long. He closed the space between us and pulled me into his arms.

"I want to do something with you. I've dreamed of it since the first time I saw you. You were so young and innocent, then it made my need for you... for this, stronger than I had ever felt. But we won't play this way unless you agree."

"What do you want to do?"

"I want to chase you."

"Here?"

"Yes, through the woods and when I catch you... when I catch you I want to fuck you," he growled into my ear. The sound vibrated something deep within me, causing my body to quiver with need.

"You want to chase me?"

He reached down and lifted my forearm to his mouth. I watched as he ran his tongue over the wound the branch had left behind, cleaning up the drops of blood that came to the surface. "Yes, I want to chase you, la mia bella ragazza."

I stood there for a minute thinking this through. I knew in my heart I'd never deny Nico, but the idea of running through the woods and hoping he'd catch me was something I had never considered. My heart raced at the possibilities. Would he catch me? What if I got lost? Or hurt? None of it mattered, though. I was with Nico, and the little fears that were invading my mind only made me want to play more. I wanted to run. Now.

I took a step back from him and watched the concern that crossed his face. Instead of using words, I looked up at him and smiled. Then, without warning, I turned and ran for my life.

CHAPTER FOURTEEN

NICO

That little vixen made me question myself, and now she worked her way into a head start. I didn't think she would agree this easily. In fact, I didn't even think she'd want to run today, but when she turned and I saw her little ass dive back into the tree line, I let out an animalistic scream of excitement. Her clothes made it easy for her to blend into the trees, but she was clumsy and loud so I could easily hear her.

"Baby girl, you shouldn't have taken off like that. I didn't give you permission to run," I taunted from behind her as she picked up her pace when she heard my voice, "You don't really think you can escape me, do you? These are my woods."

My heart was beating loud in my ears but I could still hear her gasping for air as the pace and excitement got to her. Today would be an easy catch, but in time I'd train her. I watched as her hair whipped around in the slight breeze and I couldn't wait to wrap it around my hand. She was quick, I'd give her credit for that. We were coming up on an area where there had been a lot of older trees. When winter came through, many had lost their fight and now lay dead in the pathway. We hit the outer edge of the wreckage and she began jumping over and onto some of the smaller branches to get through.

"That's going to slow you down, little girl. Are you sure you want to head that way?" I slacked off a bit, allowing her to work her way around a larger tree. I had her cornered already, but she wasn't willing to admit it. She jumped from stump to stump, laughing as she went. If I had any idea the amount of joy something like this would bring her, I would have talked to her about it weeks ago. Today I had hoped she'd be running on adrenaline from the kill, that the high would persuade her decision to try something new. Whether it was that or just her own little kinky mind at play didn't matter. She was my life, my love, and now my prey.

"You're not that fast!" she shouted in my direction when I stopped and watched her move her sexy little body under another fallen tree.

"Oh, you don't think so?"

"No!" she shouted as she worked her way further down the hill. I couldn't see her anymore, but I wanted to give her the lead. Time was lost on me. We could have been running for a few minutes or an hour at this point. The only thing consuming my consciousness was Valentina. My cock was so fucking hard it hurt and my balls were protesting the run. I climbed over the fallen trees and peered over the side, assuming I'd see her running towards the next clearing, but she was gone.

I stood still, trying to hear what direction she had moved in. There wasn't a sound out of place. Birds sang, and the rustling of leaves from the surrounding trees were the only noises I could hear.

"Valentina!" I shouted, hoping beyond hope she would respond. How did I lose her? She wasn't even that far ahead of me.

"Valentina!" I tried again, but only the silence of her missing was heard. Panic set in. Something had to have been wrong. I knew my way around these woods as well as I knew my way around our own house. If she went straight through, she'd reach the smaller clearing. To the left is the stream which was probably dried up and to the right was thick brush. The only way that made sense was straight ahead, but she didn't know that. I looked around again, trying to see if I had missed something, anything that would clue me in as to which direction she went, but there was nothing.

"Valentina, I'm not playing anymore. If you hear me, come back this way." My voice carried into the void. Nothing.

I moved forward towards the clearing I knew was ahead as my mind raced toward every worst-case scenario. No one was out here. This was our private land. It's not like someone could have come and taken her from me. Not again. The fear drove me to run faster. I ignored the pain in my chest that wasn't from the run but the thought of losing her again. I was less than five feet away from the grassy area when I heard it. Someone was behind me.

I stopped and turned, expecting to see my nightmares come to life, someone here to kill me after they had taken my heart. But it wasn't my nightmare, it was my sassy little girl lunging for me. Her small body propelled through the air, leaving me just enough time to reach out and catch her. My fear and panic had me unsteady on my feet and we went tumbling to the ground. I was furious, but the smile on her face and joy in her eyes made it hard for me to scream. I leaned forward and sunk my teeth into her neck as she screamed and ground her hips into me.

"I caught you," she gasped, "I caught you."

She did, but there was no way in hell I'd admit she got me at my own game. Not now anyway. I pushed her off of me and reached for her shirt, tearing it from her body with a force fueled by my anger with myself. I shouldn't have let my anxiety get the best of me, I shouldn't have thought the worst. My little girl was safe. We would never let anything happen to her again. She hadn't bothered with a bra, which left her breasts bare to me. I leaned forward and bit her nipple so hard she screamed in pain. My hands went for her jeans and I undid them, yanking them down to her ankles and leaving them there. I flipped her little body over and she got to her hands and knees. That wouldn't be enough. I needed more.

I pressed her chest down until her arms went out to her side and her face was flat against the dirt. "That's better, you filthy little slut. Do you feel the cold dirt against your cheek? A dirty face for a dirty girl."

She moaned and pushed her ass back in my direction. Degradation wasn't always my thing, but since my girl loved it, I'd give it to her. I'd give her anything.

I kneeled in behind her, I undid my jeans and pulled out my cock. The sound of my zipper was loud in the quiet woods, and my sweet girl whimpered with need.

I grabbed her hips and forced myself into her dripping center until I couldn't go any further.

"Yes! Yes!" she cried out as I pulled back and slammed into her again.

"Is this what you want?"

"Yes, more, please, fuck me, Nico. Please."

I loved the sound of her begging me. Her need for me matched only by my own for her.

"You deserved to be punished, la mia bella ragazza. You changed the rules of my game, you disobedient little girl."

Valentina's body was damp with sweat from the run. I reached forward and pulled her to me by her hair. Her legs were barely parted because of the restraint of her jeans, and the movement only caused her cunt to squeeze me tighter. I pressed myself into her again and again as I held her to me. She was close, but I needed more. I pushed her forward and pulled out, much to her dismay. My t-shirt was slick with sweat and pissing me off, so I pulled it from my body and threw it to the side. I turned my sweet girl over and removed her shoes and what was left of her clothes.

Looking down at her gorgeous body in the dirt and leaves made me want to yell out in happiness. She was everything I could have ever wished for. She lifted her knees and opened her beautiful folds to me. I bent down and dipped my tongue into her center, slowly licking my way up to her ready little clit.

"Fuck, Nico. I need you."

"Tell me then, I want to hear it."

"Fuck me, hard. I want your cock back inside me. Fuck me so hard it hurts, press me into this dirt and show me who owns me."

Her words undid me. She reached her hands out to her sides and dug her nails into the ground as I covered my body with hers. I lifted one leg and slid deep inside her, the movement making her back arch up just off the ground. This was it. Pure ecstasy. I watched as her body moved with mine like it had been made just for me. Her eyes looked up into mine as if nothing in the world existed outside of the two of us. Thrust after thrust, she met me again and again until her lips parted and she groaned in pleasure. I could feel it coming just as easily as I felt it hit. Like an explosion from deep within her core, her pussy grabbed my cock and pulled me tighter. Her back arched up and her head fell back, as she reached for me to ground her while wave after wave crashed into her body. I held her to me when it was over, pumping into her only a few more times as my body rewarded hers with the sweet release of my passion for her.

We stayed like that for far longer than was necessary. Valentina had wrapped her legs and arms around me as if she was holding on for dear life. The feel of her body beneath mine would never get old. It didn't matter how I touched her, or how we laid together, she had quickly become my drug of choice.

When I rolled onto my back, I took her with me and placed my hand behind her head to lay her down on my chest. She was filthy, covered in dirt that had turned into a pasty mud from our sweat and cum. There were small twigs and leaves matted in her hair and a smile on her face as she closed her eyes.

"I got you," she whispered.

"You got me."

When we had enough of the bugs, I helped her to her feet. Since I hadn't planned well, we had nothing to clean up with other than her torn shirt, which I used to clean the mess between her legs before I helped her back into her jeans. My shirt was a wreck, but I didn't think Dante would appreciate us making our way back to the house with her both shirtless and braless, so I slid it over her head and placed a kiss on her nose.

"Here, this way we won't get into too much trouble," I said with a smirk.

"We are not going to get into trouble. I told them both today that I was tired of them interfering in our relationship."

I reached for her hand as we began our walk back. "Oh, you did, did you?"

"I did, and I have no problem withholding sex from them if they chose not to comply."

I laughed, "I see."

"There are some benefits to having three boyfriends, you know. My needs still get met when one of you fucks up."

"Boyfriends, huh?"

She stopped and looked up at me, "That's what you are, right? I didn't mean to assume anything."

"No, Valentina, I'm not your boyfriend. I don't think the word explains what we have correctly. I'm uncertain there is a word that does, maybe soulmate? But that sounds like some corny shit Ares would say. All I know is you are my world, so if boyfriend is what you want to call me until I can call you wife, then that's fine."

Her eyes went wide, and I leaned in to kiss her.

"Wife?"

"Of course, you didn't think we wouldn't marry you, did you?"

"But how?"

I pulled her forward, so we kept moving. "I have no idea, but we'll figure it out. You are our Queen and we're never going to let you go. I know you were promised to Dante, but you've chosen all of us. If you want a big ass fancy wedding someday, I'm sure Ares will help you plan it. If you want a million kids running around, then we will give you that too. You can have anything you want from us. All you have to do is ask."

Valentina was quiet after I spoke. Not uncomfortably so. She seemed content in what I had shared. I know we had grown close at an alarming rate and things were moving along with Ares and Dante as well, but I realized as we walked that none of us communicated the future with her very well. We told her she would be ours forever, but I don't think anyone ever told her she could have a normal life she had dreamed of with weddings, kids and friends. This was all so new for each of us, but she needed to know she could have it all if she wanted.

When we stepped out of the tree line and onto the grassy knoll of the backyard she came to a stop. "I want a small wedding, just us here at the house so we can all exchange vows. Dante's cousins can come and your friend Anton with his wife. Maybe a few others, but nothing crazy, okay?"

"Okay, anything else?"

"I want kids. At least one with each of you, but I'm not ready for that now."

I smiled down at her and pulled her into my arms. "Kids, got it."

She smiled up at me, "That doesn't weird you out."

"A little, but not because I don't want to have a baby with you. In fact, the thought of you round with my child does things to me that are rather distracting," I said as I pressed my semi-hard dick into her.

She laughed, "You really are unbelievable."

"What can I say? You just do it for me."

"If it's not that, then what is it?"

I stepped back, letting her go. I reached for her hand and started up to the house. "They diagnosed me with a lot of mental health issues over the years. Now that I know Alessia is alive, it feels different, but that doesn't mean it's all gone. When the time comes to make decisions about starting our family, I will meet with a doctor. I want to know the risks of our child inheriting any of this from me."

"Nico, I—"

"Shh... don't say anything, la mia bella ragazza. I'm sure it will be fine. Before we make a decision, I just want us to know," I said looking over at her as we ascended the steps that lead up to the house.

"I love you," she whispered as I reached for the door.

"I love you too. Now come on, we need a shower and then I have to go clean up a body."

CHAPTER FIFTEEN

VALENTINA

I sat at a table surrounded by more men than I had been around in my entire life. Today was the meeting Anton had set up for Dante and I was shocked when he told me I would be attending. All eyes had been on me since I walked into the room. Most had looks on their faces filled with judgement, but a few of the younger members smirked and seemed amused that Dante had brought me. The choice he had made wasn't normal, women, unless they were the head of their own family, did not attend things like this. In New York city, men ran all the families.

Ironically enough, I learned from Ares the more progressive families weren't even in the United States.

"Thank you all for coming," Dante started as everyone took a seat.

Nico had put me in the seat between Dante and Ares, and he stood behind me. I couldn't help but think I was taking his place, but he didn't seem to care. Anton was next to Ares, but other than that, the only people I knew were old acquaintances of my father and the sons of those men.

"We have a situation that we need to discuss and I felt it was best to do it face to face."

A few men nodded their heads. "As you know, we have recently uncovered a great deal of information about a group of people looking to gain power in our city. The individual who is leading this ascension is someone who you all know. Mario Romano has been working against the Corsetti Family for some time and it is ending now. Long before we took Valentina, he had made moves with the Costa family to gain power. Right under the noses of all of you."

I watched as some men grumbled and others fidgeted uncomfortably in their seats. "Let me assure you we already know who each of you are that entertained the idea of working with him, and we will address each of you individually. Mario Romano is spreading hate across this city. He is crossing lines with local gangs, and the biker community, hoping to unite them under his rule. It's not working. Our partners throughout the city are loyal, more so than a few of you. They have refused him. Mario Romano will die."

"What about the Costas?" Michael Bartolomeo asked.

"If you haven't heard, Angelo's son was recently found dead from an overdose. His father is currently mourning the death of his only child while awaiting trial for human trafficking."

"So he's out?"

"Yes."

People leaned over, whispering to one another as Dante sat and watched.

"What's your plan for him?"

"Angelo's sins fall far beyond that of human trafficking. A life in prison will not suffice. Trust we will handle him as we see fit."

A few heads nodded around the room. "My purpose in bringing you here today is twofold. First, I expect those of you who had planned to turn against me now know your fate will be the same as that of your dear friend Mario. Second, if anything happens to our Queen again, I will burn the city down and start over. I don't give a fuck about how many years of service your family has with mine. No one gets to her again. If you have a problem with any of this, you are welcome to leave New York."

I stared up at Dante, shocked by his words. A man like him would never risk his family and business for a woman. At least I hadn't thought he would. Was this why he wanted me here? To prove to me I was worth it all? I didn't realize I was holding my breath until I felt Nico's hand come down on my shoulder. It startled me at first, then I relaxed under his touch. Dante reached for my hand before continuing.

"Valentina Romano is the future of the Corsetti Family. She will breathe life into our future generation and will be protected at all costs."

Heads nodded, and some spoke up with congratulations. Dante didn't leave these men with a choice. The Dark Kings rose to power long before I came into the picture. Dante played the politics well, keeping peace between everyone at this table, which earned him the respect his grandfather had once had. Families complied under his father's rule but only out of respect for the man that started it all. I smiled, proud of the man Dante had become and the person he chose to be.

"I have one last thing to share before we leave today. Alessia De Bartoli will arrive soon. She will be a guest of ours at the Corsetti estate. I am certain I don't need to express the importance of her respect and protection while she is in our city. Each of you will accept her graciously and if she is not, I will allow her to choose your fate. The alliance we have with the De Bartoli Empire lasts longer than any of us and it will be respected while she is Stateside."

"I thought she was dead." One of the younger men spoke up while looking at Nico. I reached up and placed my hand over his.

"I can assure you, she is very much alive."

"Isn't she the one who took Valentina?" A loud-mouthed kid who I didn't know spoke up. An older man who was sitting next to him rewarded the kid with a smack on the back of his head.

"Don Corsetti, I apologize for my son's outburst. He is learning his place."

The younger man at least had the decency to look embarrassed.

"It's fine, Ricky. She is the one who protected Valentina. We owe her a debt."

As soon as things started, they were over. Some men began filing out of the room while others stayed behind. Dante, Ares and I stood but didn't leave. People had lined up to speak with Dante. Many offered well wishes on our future, others had additional questions or requests for meetings, which Ares handled. The entire time they spoke, Dante stood with me next to him. His hand on my back was the only thing keeping me still and damping my desire to run. When the last person left the room, he turned and looked at me.

"You behaved very well today, Ragazzina. So well, in fact, you may choose your own reward."

It didn't take me long to think about it. I smiled up at him. "I want to go on a date."

"A date?"

"Yes," I said, smiling up at him, "A fancy dinner date with all of you."

Ares laughed, and Nico smiled, rolling his eyes at Dante's expression. "A date it is, then." He immediately turned to Ares. "Maybe that little place that Gina's friend just opened up. Do you think you could call and get us a table tonight?"

"Sure."

We walked out of the meeting room that had housed all the families. It was attached to an old Italian restaurant that probably was built before half the city even existed. As we moved through the restaurant, I saw small groups of people watching us. Many were families we had just met with, others were simply customers of the restaurant. I wasn't sure why, but rather than being shy over the stares, they seemed to build me up. I stood tall between my men, proud of who they were and who I was to them. They were my future, and I was theirs. I had no question about that now. Not after my conversation with Nico, and certainly not after Dante's meeting today. It would have been nice if he had told me before announcing it to the families of the city, but that wasn't how he did things. The choices he made today were a declaration of love, whether or not he wanted to admit it, and I wasn't going to pick it apart.

Later that night, we were sitting inside a small but gorgeous restaurant. There was a private room that had been reserved for the four of us and I hadn't been somewhere so nice since my father was alive. Except back then he was dragging me around to places I didn't want to go. I ran my hand over the pressed white tablecloth and realized how different my life was. In the past, I would dread meals like this, but tonight I was excited about good food and time with my men.

"Do you know what you want?" Ares asked, leaning over and looking at my menu that I still hadn't picked up.

"Hmmm... maybe some pasta. What are you getting?"

"A steak."

"That's it?"

"Ah, no. Between the three of us, I wouldn't be surprised if we order half the menu. We haven't been out in a long time and everyone says the food here is amazing."

"I'm sorry about that. I guess you haven't been out because of me."

Ares winked, "It's okay. I think we all prefer feeding you while you're naked in bed to taking you out and sharing you with the world."

My laugh caught the attention of Dante, who was sitting across from me. "He's right, you know. My desire to leave the house is less and less every day."

"I'm surprised you are willing to admit that," I said, reaching for my wine.

"Why do you say that?"

"Honestly? Because until today I didn't know how you felt about me. I mean, I know you care about me, but today was... surprising."

While I waited for Dante to say something, I ignored the quiet stares of Ares and Nico. "I didn't mean to confuse you. I thought I had been very clear that you are ours and we'd do anything to protect you."

"I understand that. But to risk the business for me? That was surprising."

He reached forward for my hand. "Ragazzina, you are my life, much in the same way my grandmother was for my grandfather. You come above all else, and I don't want you to ever question that."

My smile was hard to contain. "I love you too."

Dante leaned back and smirked at me while Ares and Nico tried to contain their laughter until the waitress walked in to take our order.

The food was amazing and I was running on a high I couldn't explain. It's not like I had ever been on a date before so I didn't know what to expect, and even if I had it wouldn't have offered me much experience since I wasn't in a relationship with one man, I was dating three.

"Nico tells me you want a family," Dante said, making me nearly spit out the wine I had just taken a sip of.

I looked over at the man in question and shot him an evil look as he just smiled as if he had done nothing wrong.

"Okay, I get that there are no secrets between the three of you, but how in the world do you communicate so well when I'm always with you? Is there a secret group text that I'm not on titled: What I did with Valentina today?"

Ares reached for my hand. "Yes. That's exactly what it is. Especially because Nico is so good with technology."

"Oh, come on, I can use my damn phone."

"Really? Because out of the three of us, I've replaced yours more times than I can count."

"It's not my fault they don't last long."

I loved it when they were all like this. These carefree moments of them just being themselves around me were things I cherished. It was so often that they were forced to put on these fronts of men who were built of steel and emotionless. It had to be exhausting.

I reached over and placed a hand on Nico's thigh. "Yes, I will admit that I always imagined myself as a mother. I want to be clear that it's not something I'm ready for right now, but it is something I want in our future."

"One from each of us?" Ares asked, even though I had a feeling he already knew the answer.

"Yes, or more. That's something we can figure out when the time comes. Is that something each of you would want?" I said, looking between Dante and Ares since I already knew what Nico would say.

"Yes, I've always wanted a large family. I just hoped that you did, too," Ares answered first.

I looked at Dante, who seemed to avoid my eyes. "Dante? Is children something you want from me?"

"If it's what you want, then I will give it to you."

"That's not what I asked."

He took a sip from the scotch he had been swirling around in his glass. "I will be honest with you. I always assumed we would have children because I wanted to pass everything we had built down to them someday."

"But now?"

"Now things feel different. I don't know if this is the life I want our children to live, so my reasons for wanting a family with you are changing."

I didn't know how to respond, so I didn't. If I had understood him right then did that mean he wanted to step down from running New York? The worst part of this realization wasn't what he said. It was that neither Nico nor Ares seemed the least bit surprised by his revelation.

CHAPTER SIXTEEN

DANTE

"Ragazzina, wake up. I want to take you somewhere," I whispered into my little sleeping beauty's ear, trying my best not to wake Nico since he would only delay our departure. She moaned and stretched into my arms. I reached for her and scooped her up from between Nico and Ares. I had woken up early and felt restless. With us all hovering so close, it was hard to pull her away, but I needed some time alone with her. I knew Nico and Ares wouldn't mind, but she seemed to be in the best spirits when we were all together, so for now, we stuck by that plan. Her time away from us was short, but it left a lasting impression.

I carried her from her room into mine and set her down on her feet. She was adorably sleepy with her messy bun and one of Ares' band t-shirts hanging down to her knees.

"Where are we going?" she mumbled as she turned for the bathroom.

"It's a surprise. I laid out clothes for you by the sink."

One of the many things I adored about this woman was how, when she wanted to, she could follow instructions perfectly. It didn't take her long to shower, change, and be ready to go. While she did, I went down to the kitchen and got her coffee in a to-go mug. As she stepped from the bathroom, I held it out to her greedy hands.

"Mmmm... I needed this," she moaned as she took a sip.

"I know. Now come on," I said, pulling her behind me.

"What's the rush?"

"The pilot's been waiting for over an hour."

"Pilot?"

We went out the side entrance that opened to our helicopter pad. I didn't use it often, truthfully I wasn't a huge fan of the metal contraption, but when I wanted to get into the city quickly or out to the Hamptons, it was nice to have. The second Valentina saw it parked and waiting for us, she jumped into my arms, with the excitement of a small child who had just walked into a candy shop.

"Is that for us?"

"It is."

"Where are we going?"

"You'll see. Come on, they've been waiting."

We made our way into the helicopter and I reached over to buckle her and place headphones on her ears. She had a look of wonder on her face that warmed my insides.

I pointed at the headphones. "This is how we will talk through the ride. Can you hear me okay?"

"Yes!"

Her excitement overrode most of my anxiety. The pilot took us over the city, flying by a bunch of the touristy stuff for her benefit..

"I've never been there," Valentina said as she pointed to Lady Liberty out the window. "I've never done much of anything in the city outside of museums."

"We'll have to change that someday."

She pulled her gaze from the window and looked over at me. "You'd really do that for me? Because I want to see all of it. Broadway, The Statue of Liberty, The Empire State Building, even the 9/11 Memorial."

"Yes, of course. We will take you to all of it," I said with a laugh, "But if you want to go to Coney Island, Ares is taking you. That place gives me the creeps."

"Oh really? Mr. Dark and Deadly himself is scared of Coney Island?"

"I didn't say I was scared. It's just gross, so make sure you bathe thoroughly before climbing into bed that night."

Valentina went to lean forward with her lips pressed together but her seatbelt wouldn't give, and she pouted. I chuckled at her disappointment until she went back to enjoying the city passing alongside of us. She was taking in everything around her, and the reality of her upbringing set in. I had always known she was sheltered, but when she shared all the things she never did, I realize how much she missed out on. Breakfast for dinner, even picking out things online that she wanted to buy, were all new experiences for her. I still chastised Ares for showing her how to use Amazon, but he'd just laugh and tell me she deserved it. Which she did.

"Valentina?"

"Yeah?" she said, turning back to me.

"When we get back to the house tonight, I want you to make a list of everything you have ever wanted to do. I don't care how big or small it is. Want to see the Eiffel Tower? Write it down. Want to carve a pumpkin? Write that down too. I want a list of everything so Nico, Ares and I can make sure you never miss out on anything again."

Her smile said more than any words could have. I lifted her hand to my lips and placed a soft kiss on the inside of her wrist just as we were landing. I pulled her headphones from her and unbuckled her seatbelt as the pilot came around to open her door.

"Thanks, Ricardo," I said, shaking the man's hand, "We'll be ready to head back later this afternoon."

"No problem, boss."

I reached for Valentina and helped her down. Her arms came around my waist as she stood before me on her tiptoes. I bent to her, letting her lips touch mine. A bolt of heat ran through me as it always did when she initiated anything.

"Come on, I have some things I want you to see."

She followed close behind me, taking in the property that surrounded us. I reached for the backdoor but stopped when Valentina pulled my arm back.

"Wait, whose house are we at?"

"Ours, well... Yours."

"What?"

"Come on, I'll show you."

She was hesitant, but followed me in. I had to pull her with me and make sure she didn't walk into anything since her eyes were busy taking everything in. I planned to start in the kitchen, since that's where I had asked our attorney to wait for us.

"Mr. Corsetti, it's always good to see you," Christy Calvano said as we approached and her hand reached out to mine.

"It's good to see you too, Christy, and please let's stick with Dante."

She nodded, then turned to my little beauty. "You must be Valentina. I've heard a lot about you."

"I wish I could say the same," she said with a smile.

"I take it Dante didn't let you in on his plans for today?"

"No, he sure did not."

"Are you one that likes surprises? Personally, I hate them, but my husband seems to always think they are a good idea."

"I guess it depends on what the surprise is," she said, looking back at me.

"Let's have a seat." I gestured to the oversized kitchen table where Christy was already set up at.

Valentina settled in and I asked Christy for a minute alone to explain what I had in store for her. "This property belonged to my grandmother. My grandfather had put it in the name of a business that she was the sole owner of. When she passed, he put that business in my name. It's the only property I own without Nico and Ares. However, this place holds their childhood memories as much as it does mine. When we were young, we spent every summer out here. Nico never had any family to speak of, and Ares spent most of his teenage years rebelling against the world.

This was the one place we could come to escape the chaos of my father and his business. It was just as much of a home to us as the property upstate and the one in Sicily. Over the years, we have acquired a lot of real estate, but these three properties are home. My grandfather never intended for this house to be mine. I've only been holding it for the woman I'd fall in love with. That woman is you."

I reached up and wiped a stray tear from her eye. "You really love me?"

"Yes, I never expected to fall in love with you. After growing up with my father, I had lost hope that marriage even worked, but now with you in our lives, it's impossible to deny how much you have changed us, changed me."

I leaned back as she stood and climbed into my lap. I loved the feel of her in my arms and when she leaned over and whispered in my ear, I realized how deep that love ran.

"I love you, Dante Corsetti. I think I loved the idea of you for my whole life, but now that I know the person you are, I could never live a day without you."

She held me to her tightly, and I responded the only way I knew how, "I love you too, my beautiful little girl."

"Sorry to interrupt, but my friend Hope just called and I need to head back to the city."

"Is everything okay?" Valentina asked as she climbed off me, "Yes, everything's fine. It appears their dog, Loki, tore up one of my daughter's favorite toys and she's having a meltdown."

Valentina laughed. "Oh, my!"

"You know, there was a point in my life where I got to wear fancy suits like this all day and I had people who valued my opinion on things. Now, I'm about to rush off to the city because my big manly husband can't take it when his baby girl is crying her eyes out."

Valentina's laugh lit up the room. I watched as the two women joked about both me and Christy's husband, Jason. I hoped beyond anything else that we could provide Valentina with a life that kept a smile on her face like she had today. One filled with friends, family and love.

Christy took a seat and explained the documents to her as she signed. Most people would think I was insane gifting her a seventy-five million dollar home, but I never looked at this property as mine. Ever since the day my father told me I'd marry Valentina, this property was hers. When we finished, she and I walked Christy out front and to her waiting car. She was one of the most efficient real estate attorneys in the city and when she left the firm, she worked at, Ares tracked her down and nearly begged her to keep us on as a client. I've learned over the years when you find a person who is fantastic at what they do, you try your best to hold on to them.

"You know, if you hadn't just given me an entire house I may be jealous of that one," Valentina said as we watched Christy's driver pull out.

"Oh, really?"

"Um... yeah. Did you see her ass? That woman is gorgeous."

I laughed and pulled her to my side. "The only ass I want to spank is yours, little girl. Come on, let me show you around."

It took a while to walk her through the entire property. It was one of the largest homes we owned, but also one of the oldest. There were over fifteen bedrooms, many of which had been closed off for years. Valentina had ideas for each of them, not to mention some of the other outdated rooms in the main part of the house.

"I don't want to change too much and lose the feel of this place. It's clear your grandmother had a gorgeous vision in mind, and I want to uphold that."

"Yes, but feel free to lose the pink striped wallpaper in the sitting room."

"Got it, no pink stripes."

Her laugh had become an addiction for me, and I just couldn't pull my eyes from her. "You really are perfect."

"You know that's not even a little bit true. But we could pretend just for now." She reached for my neck and I leaned down. Instead of kissing her, I lifted her up and she wrapped her legs around my waist.

"Come on, there is one last thing I want to show you."

"What's that?"

"Our bedroom."

I made my way down the long hallway that opened up to the master suite and stepped inside with Valentina in my arms. She gasped at the view of the water and I couldn't blame her. Almost every wall of this house had a window, but the floor to ceiling glass I had installed when we redid this room made it feel as if we were in another world. I laid her on the bed and covered her body with mine.

"Will you help me break in our new bed?"

She looked around and then back up at me. "This is new?"

"All of it. The house is older and the original master would never fit us all. I had the construction started about a year ago and they finished while we were in Sicily. Do you like it?"

"I love it."

"Good."

I stood and stripped out of my clothes. Before I could even get to her, Valentina had already taken off her jeans and was messing with her shirt. I reached for it and pulled it from her body along with the tiny thong and lace bra she was wearing. Still, to this day, I found it entertaining that nearly everything she wore had been picked out by Ares. Even when she started ordering things to be delivered to the house, it was never clothes. Mostly books and silly gadgets she thought were interesting. There were some things for the kitchen and a ton of gag gifts for Ares, but never new clothes.

"Why don't you ever buy clothes for yourself?"

"I don't know. I mean, I like everything Ares got for me and I've never had so many clothes in my life, so I certainly don't need anymore."

"I want you to change anything you don't like. Clothes, the houses, anything. Just promise me you won't always just take things as they are to make us happy."

Her small smile pulled me in, and I crawled onto the bed, spreading her open for me. "Enough talking about houses and clothes. I want to taste that sweet little pussy of yours."

CHAPTER SEVENTEEN

VALENTINA

There are some days I wake up and I still can't believe this is my life. Today was one of those days. Over the last few months that we have all been together I have fallen head over heels in love with three men, learned more about myself than I ever thought possible and managed to make friends with a woman who runs one of the most dangerous crime families in all of Sicily. Since Ares got me my own phone and computer, it has been easy to stay in touch with Alessia. She was looking forward to her time here in the States but it was taking a while to get everything in order.

Our first few conversations comprised her complaining about Massimo making her go to therapy and insisting she was fine. But recently her thoughts on it all had changed, and I felt bad for how much she was struggling with the reality that she wasn't doing very well after all.

"You're sure you want her here, staying with us?" Nico asked for what had to be the hundredth time.

"Yes. I'm looking forward to it, but like I've said before, if you are uncomfortable with her coming, she will make other arrangements."

"No, it's fine. I mean, if you're fine with it then I am too."

I turned from the mirror in my bathroom where I was trying to get ready for tonight and walked to where he was standing. "Tell me the truth, Nico, if this is too much, my feelings won't be hurt. I know you both have a difficult past and you've made so much progress, I don't want to set you back."

"I'm okay. Really, I am."

"Good." I reached up and pulled him down to my level, placing a kiss on his lips. "Now, go find something to do until I'm ready. You know how aggravated Dante gets when we are late, because you distracted me."

"One last thing," he said as he bent down on one knee and ran his hands up my leg to my inner thigh.

"Nico!" I laughed as he hovered a little too close for comfort before reaching for my panties and pulling them down my legs.

"These are mine," he said as he lifted them to his nose, then placed them in his pocket, "And don't even think about covering yourself with another pair. I want easy access to you tonight."

He straightened and walked from the bathroom as I stood there speechless with a throbbing clit and an ache that never seemed to leave while he was around. I finished getting ready because what I said was true. Whenever we were late because of Nico and I, Dante spent most of the night pouting like an overgrown child, which then caused Ares to make jokes all night that just worsened the situation.

I reached for my bag and nearly ran out to the main part of the house when I looked at the time. We were heading to the club tonight and I couldn't wait to get there. The guys had been busier than usual, each with their own things. Dante had issues with one of the buildings they own in the financial district, so he had been there working with a construction firm most of the week. Ares was hiring three new artists for the shop because of an expansion, and Nico seemed to be my designated babysitter. Not that I was complaining. A hot tattoo-covered man who preferred to spend the day in bed with me versus working was not a bad thing.

I got to the foyer and found Ares waiting. "Ready?"

"Is he mad?"

"No more angry than usual," he said, lowering his head to kiss me before opening the front door. We always took a minimum two cars to most places, but tonight I noticed three.

"Who am I riding with?"

"Me. Nico has to head out after the meeting, and Dante wants to make sure I can take you home whenever you are ready."

The meeting. It was the one thing I had been dreading for weeks. Ares had finally tracked down my cousin and I would meet with him tonight. There were a lot of things I wanted to say to him, but I had been warned not to scare him off. The difficulties he had drummed up between families had gotten better, but since he had been reaching out to people outside of the Corsetti's control, a certain level of politics was still at play.

As we descended the steps, I ran my hand along my upper thigh. Nico had gifted me a new knife with a custom leather thigh holster made just for it. I wore it high enough that you couldn't see it under the skirt of my dress, but until I proved to Ares I could shoot, he refused to give me a gun. In a few days time that would change. He planned a surprise for me, but Nico couldn't keep it to himself. I smiled as I thought back on the day Ares told me he was taking me out. He was so excited and only moments later Nico came in and asked when we were going shooting. Ares didn't speak to him for the rest of the day. Living with three men who had spent nearly their entire lives together was never boring.

When we got to The Social, we entered through the back and came up the elevator just as we had done many times before. Tonight, the club was open to the public, which was rare when we showed up. Dante preferred to pick the people around him and I couldn't blame him for that, especially after what happened the last time I met with Mario. Tonight, the plan was different. Mario was still trying to play the role of an innocent man who had been taken advantage of, and we were letting him think we believed him. The idea of leaving the club open to the public was Ares'. He thought Mario would be more willing to show up knowing the club was full of strangers rather than crime families and acquaintances of the Corsettis.

"Damn, girl, you're looking fine!" Gina said as she pulled me into a hug. Dante's cousin was one of those people that just pulled you in. She was always so busy with the club that we rarely got to spend time together, but I liked knowing that if we did, we would become good friends.

"Thank you. It's so nice being out of the house. These guys have been slammed lately and if I didn't have the garden and food to cook, I'd be bored out of my mind."

"Hey, I keep you busy," Nico said with a look of insistence on his face.

I patted his shoulder. "Yes, dear. You keep me very busy."

I rolled my eyes as Gina laughed, "I set The Jezebel Room up for you all and I have a meeting room downstairs ready for Mario. Your guards have already been through it and they are waiting for you there. I also have club security closing the doors when the meeting starts," she turned to me and added, "Nothing will happen to you this time. We've made sure of it."

"I know Gina. Everything will be fine."

The first time I had seen her when we got back, she was a mess of emotions. For a woman like her to crack, I knew it was hard. She took on a lot of blame when none of what happened that night was her fault.

"I could use a drink. Anyone else?" Ares said, reaching for my hand and pulling me from the room.

"I'll be out in a few minutes. I'm going to go downstairs and talk to security," Dante added, as Nico followed us from the office into the club.

The ambiance of a nightclub was unreal. Considering The Social was the only one I had been to, I felt a little spoiled. It was nothing like what you saw on TV. There was no smelly bar and cringey lights. The Social was a gathering place for the richest of the rich and walking through it in the early hours made that clear. Lots of fancy men in suits with women hanging off their every word crowded the tables and bars. There were three dance floors but only the main was truly crowded. Ares kept his hand on my back as we followed Nico to the private area Gina had set up for us. There were already four of our men there, standing watch. I had gotten used to most of them, a few refused to even smile and it still annoyed me, but Dante assured me it didn't matter if they smiled, only if they kept me alive.

One of them unhooked a velvet rope as we approached, and we made our way in. Before long, I had a drink in my hand as the music pumped through the speakers and vibrated my insides. Ares was handling the random people who always seemed to come up with a greeting or a question while Nico stood behind me, running his hands over my body and I swayed in his arms. Music was one of the many things that were Ares' passions, not so much Nico's, but he would take any opportunity he could to be close to me and I loved it.

"Are you okay?" Ares said as he turned back to check on me.

"I'm fine!" I yelled over the music, holding my glass up, showing him how good I was really doing. He smiled and my knees went weak. All of my men were fine, but it was unfair how hot Ares was. I eyed two blondes headed straight for him and immediately I knew they were going to be a problem. I stepped forward right as they reached the ropes and slipped my hand around his waist as one guard put a hand out to stop them from getting closer.

"Hey, hands off creep!" Blondie number one yelled as she pulled her arm from the man, "I'm here to see Ares. He'll tell you."

Ares' body tensed as he looked toward me before answering the pleading look on the woman's face. "It's fine. Let her through."

"Monkey! I've missed you!" she cried out as she held her arms out to pull Ares into a hug. He didn't move, and it left her standing there like a fool until she pretended like she was fixing her hair. "It's been so long since we've seen each other."

"Hello, Ann Marie."

I felt Nico's hand on my back but couldn't pull my eyes from the train wreck in front of me.

"So, are you going to invite us up for a drink? I brought Andrea. She can keep Nico busy."

The wink the woman gave was comical. She had so much makeup on, her fake eyelashes stuck together. I couldn't help but laugh. This woman had some balls. Ares' arm came around me the second she got close and he hadn't moved. If nothing else, he had pulled me closer once she started talking.

"That's not a good idea tonight. Why don't the two of you head over to the bar? I'm sure Miguel can take care of you."

"But I don't want Miguel, I want you," she said as she reached out and her finger tapped Ares' chest.

Something inside me snapped. Before she could yank her hand away, I caught it and pulled her so close to me her face was only inches from mine.

"He said no," I growled in the most unladylike manner ever.

Neither Ares nor Nico made any effort to stop me, so I pushed on. "If I catch your skanky little hands on him again, I'll break your fucking fingers. Do you understand?"

The laugh that came from her was a nervous chatter that meant nothing to me. "And you can tell your bitch-ass friend no one but me entertains Nico." I pushed her back out of my space and stepped back into their arms as if nothing had happened.

She stumbled on her heels but caught herself before she fell and straightened her dress. That was when she made the biggest mistake of her life. She turned to leave, reaching for her friend's hand, but rather than gracefully walking away, she turned and looked back at me.

"Whore!"

Everyone near us got quiet and I swear if the music wasn't still playing, you could hear a pin drop. When she turned back around, she walked right into Dante's grasp. His hand came up so quickly I didn't even see it move. Two of the guards stepped up on either side of him as he gripped Ann Marie's neck so hard she was gasping for air.

"What did you just call my Queen?" he asked in the calmest voice I had ever heard. Calm yet terrifying. When she didn't answer, he shook her body until she cried out. "I said, what did you just call my Queen?"

"A whore," she squeaked out before he dropped her and let her fall to the ground. Her hands went up around her neck as she took in large, gasping breaths of air. Dante leaned over her and whispered something in her ear I couldn't hear. If I had thought she had a look of terror on her face as he strangled her, it was nothing compared to now. She was pale as a ghost, which said a lot considering the amount of makeup she was wearing.

"Take them away," he said as he stood to his full height and stepped over the woman as if she were nothing more than a piece of shit.

He reached for me and I stepped into his arm as he leaned down and captured my mouth with his. That burning desire that seemed to simmer constantly was stoked to life, and I wanted nothing more than to climb this man and ride him for all he was worth.

"I need you," I whispered into his ear, "I need all of you."

Dante stepped back and reached for my hand as he tilted his head to Nico and Ares. We walked back through the club and towards a door I'd never noticed before. Dante pushed in a code and opened it. When we walked in, it looked like Gina's office, only larger and more masculine. There was a glass desk with two monitors to a computer and a big screen TV behind it that was running security footage. Across from the desk were two dark leather chairs and there was a seating area and a private bar in the corner.

"What is this place?"

"My office," Dante said as he pulled me further into the room.

"I didn't know you had an office here."

"I don't come here much. I prefer to work from home since you've been with us. Now, would you like to explain to me why I just caught you threatening a random woman in the club?"

CHAPTER EIGHTEEN

ARES

The second I saw Ann Marie, and Andrea, I knew they were going to cause shit. She had tried to get my attention while I was talking to a client by dancing like an idiot nearby. When I didn't bite, it was clear she was going to push things further. What I didn't expect was for my little doll to threaten to break her right in front of me. It was so fucking hot I knew without a doubt I'd be pulling the security footage to watch it back.

"Maybe you should ask Ares and Nico why I was threatening some bitch instead of me."

"Ragazzina," Dante's voice came as a low warning as Valentina moved her hands to her hips as if she were in a standoff.

"I don't like women touching you," she said, turning on me, "Or any of you, for that matter. If they can't keep their hands to themselves, then I will teach them how."

Nico's face was comical. I swear he was going to pop a blood vessel with that damn smile. "La mia piccola bambola," I said, reaching out as I tried to calm her, "You realize none of us would ever stray, right?"

"Stray? As in fuck someone else? Jesus Ares, I didn't even think about that, but now that I have, let me be clear. I'll cut your fucking dick off if you decide you want to cheat on me. I don't even like a woman poking you in the chest. What do you think would happen if you started it? Or better yet, if you reciprocated?"

"I imagine you'd cut his dick off, wouldn't you, my little beauty?" Nico said as he walked up behind her and wrapped his arms around her center, "All Ares is trying to say is that our world revolves around you. Some of us might have a past that is questionable, but all of that is behind him."

"Him?" Dante asked with a smirk on his face.

"Well, you were nearly a priest while we waited for Valentina, and I rarely fucked a bitch, so yeah... him."

"Listen, it's not like my ex fucking kidnapped her," I said as I turned to the bar to pour us drinks.

"You know what? I don't even care," Valentina interrupted as Nico was about to lose it, "All I'm saying is, keep the bitches at an arm's length away next time."

"I only entertained them tonight to clarify that they were no longer welcome. Next time, I'll send someone else to handle it."

I reached out and handed her a vodka on the rocks, which she took way too big of a sip from before handing it back to me. "Put this on the bar, will you?"

I stood there holding her nearly empty glass like an idiot when what I should have done was what she asked. To my credit, I was thoroughly distracted by her stepping out of Nico's arms to slip her heels off and get on her knees in front of Dante.

"Now, let me show you how thankful I am for stepping in when you did," she said as she pulled his cock out.

Nico wasted no time at all as he pulled his dick out and took a seat on a chair, watching our girl get her face throughly fucked by Dante. I knocked back the rest of my drink and hers, then put the glasses on the bar. When I turned back, Dante was tucking himself away and pulling her up to him. The second her little black sequin dress rode up over her backside, I knew she was in trouble.

"Are you not wearing anything under that dress?" he growled out as he gripped her ass so hard she cried out.

"I'm wearing my knife."

"Where are your panties, little girl?"

A coy smile came over her face and her eyes darted over to Nico, who just smiled and continued jerking himself off.

"I'm not used to this level of disobedience," he said as he reached for the hem of her dress and pulled it over her head.

Valentina wasn't lying. She had nothing on other than the knife Nico gave her. Her perky little nipples tightened at the onslaught of cool air and she stood before Dante, looking up at him through lidded eyes.

"Go to Ares. You will be punished for this."

My cock twitched at the sight of her walking towards me. I loved nothing more than holding her body as it shook with need from Dante's strikes. I took a seat in the chair next to Nico and reached a hand out for Valentina. She bent over my lap like the good little girl she was and I ran my hand over her soft, velvety skin.

"Give them to me," Dante said with a hand out to Nico.

He grumbled but reached into his pocket and held out a black silk thong with gold accents on the sides.

"Open up." Dante insisted as he held them out in front of Valentina's face.

"That should keep you quiet," he said as he shoved the silky fabric into her mouth.

Valentina's hair had fallen in her face, so I gathered it up and held it in my hand. Dante went around his desk and pulled out a bottle of lube and a rattan cane. I raised my eyebrows at him, but all he did was shrug. Valentina was facing Nico, eyes wide as she watched him stroke his cock. She was so distracted that at the first impact of the cane, her entire body arched up, requiring me to hold her in place for the next.

"One," Dante's voice came as he began counting.

At twelve, he stopped. My cock was so hard it was painful underneath her. Our sweet girl had taken each hit like a champion, and when I ran my hand over the angry red welts, she didn't even cry out. Her breathing was the only outward sign anything was going on, but the second my fingers slid through her folds I was greeted with the slick, wet heat that we had all grown to love.

"She's ready," I said as I coaxed her up from where she was draped over my lap and pulled her panties from her mouth, "Go to Nico, my little doll."

She stood and went to his outstretched hands. I unbuttoned my dress shirt and reached for the lube as Valentina crawled into his lap and slid down his hard cock with a sweet sigh of relief.

"She's perfect, isn't she?" Dante said to me as we watched her body move over Nico's like they made her for him.

"Yes. She is. Feisty, and not necessarily trainable, but that makes me love her even more."

"Yeah, me too," he said with a laugh.

I looked over at him and all he did was shrug. I hadn't heard him tell her he loved her yet, but ever since their trip to the Hamptons, I could feel a shift between the two of them. We always knew she was our forever, but deep inside I worried Dante would never let her in. His guilt and fear of losing her was a struggle. Nico and I both saw it every day, but Valentina made it impossible not to love everything about her. Now it looked like he finally stopped fighting the inevitable, and that just moved us one step closer to where we all needed to be.

Valentina's cries of pleasure pulled my eyes back to her. Her entire body was bouncing up and down on Nico's cock as he gripped her hips and grunted as his release hit him and she came undone atop of him. Her body fell forward, and he held her for a minute before Dante went to her.

"Come, Ragazzina."

She lifted her head and looked up at Dante, then placed a kiss on Nico's lips before he helped her to her feet. She was going to be a mess, and we still needed to meet with Mario. I hoped Dante had considered cleanup, as well as he had considered her punishments when he stocked his office. I watched as he cleared off his desk and laid her out on it. He propped her legs up and I could see the glistening folds as they called out for my cock. Dante moved to her head and pulled his cock out. Valentina didn't waste a second as she reached for him and pulled him into her mouth.

I walked over to her and nearly lost it just looking at her. I couldn't see the welts on her ass, but knowing they were there up against the glass top of Dante's desk was more than enough. Her dark hair had fallen from the clip she had it up in and her makeup was smeared all over her face. Add to it all that her beautiful pussy was on display, and I didn't know how much more I could take.

I stepped between her legs with my cock in my hand, jerking it in long slow strokes.

"Does my little doll have an empty cunt?"

Valentina's mouth was full, but she lifted her hips in the cutest way, indicating her need for me.

"It's so messy already. Someone played with my toy and didn't clean it up," I said as I pushed the head of my cock between her wet folds and rubbed it up and down her slit, pressing it harder into her clit when I reached it.

She groaned and lifted her hips again, trying to get me to move.

"Don't worry, la mia piccola bambola. I'm going to fuck you nice and hard."

The second I told her my plans, I pushed myself into her waiting cunt and she arched her back up off the desk, reaching for me with her free hand. Dante grabbed her hair and refocused her on his cock as he thrust in and out of her mouth. I adjusted my rhythm to his pushing in and out of her again and again while she took it all like the good little girl she was.

"That's it, just like that. You are such a good girl."

She moaned again, and I could see her body blush in the excitement of her praise. Nico cleaned himself up and got dressed. He walked up and, without a second thought, leaned over and sucked her nipple into his mouth. The hand I was holding immediately went to him and she wrapped it around the back of his head, holding him in place. Her cries increased tenfold as I tried my hardest to hold off. Dante hadn't let her come again and that he let her go so freely when she was with Nico meant he was going to make her wait this time. I could feel her walls tightening around me, and I knew she was nearly there.

"She's close," I grunted out as my balls tingled in that telltale sign I didn't have much time left myself.

"Not yet," Dante ground out between his teeth, "Do not come, little girl. Not until I say so."

She tightened every muscle in her body trying to hold off the impending explosion and it just made things worse for me.

"Fuck." I thrust into her again, slower this time. Trying to hold off my climax because I wanted to feel hers when I let go.

Dante's movements were gaining speed and growing erratic. He let go of his tight hold on her hair and gently wiped away the stray strands as he looked down at her. "Ti amo piccola ragazza."

He let himself go, and I slowly fucked her as she took in every drop he gave her. When he pulled himself from her mouth, he leaned down, placed a kiss on her lips and whispered, "Now."

I didn't waste any time. She looked past Nico, who had now moved to her other breast and up at me. I picked my pace back up to the speed we were at before she was denied her pleasure. She wrapped her legs around me as Nico moved to her mouth. She ran her fingers through his hair while I held her hips and fucked her as if our lives depended on it.

Without any warning, she cried out and her body clenched around mine. She was so tight and wet it was like heaven on earth. My climax hit me in waves of pure pleasure and it wasn't until Nico pulled away and I had her in my arms that I realized how badly she must have needed this.

"I love you," I whispered as I reached for her and pulled her off the desk. With my cock still deep inside her, I held her to my body as she wrapped herself around me. "I will always love you, because I've never loved anyone else."

CHAPTER NINETEEN

VALENTINA

It took me longer than I had hoped to get cleaned up. Luckily, there was a bathroom attached to Dante's office, so I had a place to pull myself together. I could hear the three of them in the other room arguing over only god knows what. I smiled at the sound of their constant bickering. When I walked back out to the office, all three of them turned to look at me. I could feel the blush running up my body under their gaze. I was absolutely crazy for each one of them and there was no hiding it.

“Ready?” Nico asked as he came to me and placed his hand on my back.

“Yeah, let’s get this over with.”

“You’re sure I can’t kill him tonight?” he whispered in my ear as we walked out of Dante’s office and to the elevator that would take us down to the meeting rooms.

“No, I don’t want a mess in the club,” Dante said before I could even bother to answer.

I wasn’t ready for Mario to die yet. I had a million questions, and Ares still wasn’t certain who all his connections were. The elevator doors opened, and I was hit with an uncomfortable sense of déja vu. The last time I walked down this hallway was the night they took me from Nico. Tonight, however, I had all three of my men, and it looked like a small army was waiting for us at the end of the hall.

“Why are there so many guys?” I asked as we approached the group that was waiting for us.

Ares took Nico’s place as he moved into the room first. “We aren’t taking any more chances with your life.”

Dante made me and Ares wait until he went inside and called for us. Mario wasn’t there yet, or if he was, they had him somewhere else. The furniture that was in this room last time had been removed and in its place was a long conference table. I took a seat next to Dante and Ares sat on my other side while Nico paced behind us.

I wasn’t nervous, just a little on edge. Nico looked like he wanted to crawl out of his own skin, and I hadn’t seen him like that in a long time.

I leaned over and whispered to Dante, “I’m worried about him.”

“I know, Ragazzina. He will be fine. This will be over soon and we will be on our way home.”

Nico had pulled out his knife and was flipping it around. I reached for mine and ran my hand over the outline of it under my skirt. Dante was right. We just needed to get this done and get home. Then everyone would feel better.

Anton walked into the conference room. "Are you ready?"

"Yeah, bring him in," Dante said as he reached for my hand.

When Anton came back in, he was pushing Mario through the door. Four of our security guys came in with him and stood over where Anton had pushed him into his seat. I didn't even know Anton was here tonight, but I wasn't surprised. Leo and Noah probably weren't far, either. There were very few people Dante trusted to work closely with him. The three of them seemed to be pretty much it. We had a ton of men who worked security, but Anton, Leo and Noah seemed to be given the larger jobs. When this was all over, I was going to sit Dante, Ares, and Nico down and make them tell me everything. I couldn't support them in the ways they needed unless they kept me in the loop about everything. It was time.

"Sweet cousin, it's so good to see you," Mario said, gesturing for me to come to him.

"You're close enough," Nico said from behind me.

"I see," he said, looking at the man behind me with a knowing smile.

"Mario, you are only alive because Valentina has asked to speak with you. I'd watch how you handle yourself tonight," Dante said as Mario dropped his outstretched arm.

"Dante, understand I was lost when Angelo approached me. I had just suffered the death of my uncle and nearly lost my cousin. Things are different now. I have my feet under me and I'm willing to work with you all."

What the hell did he mean by that? I thought as I felt Ares caress my leg. I know he meant it for comfort, but my body was still buzzing from earlier and even with a room full of people, I could feel my core heat as his thumb ran down my inner thigh. He grinned when I looked over at him. He knew exactly what he was doing, and I was going to kick his ass for it as soon as we got home.

I turned back to my asshole cousin. "What do you mean by work with us?"

"I assume that's why we are meeting, no?"

"We are meeting because you tried to drug me and sell me back to Mateo Costa."

"Valentina, please. You know that was all a mistake, right? I knew Alessia was coming for you and that you'd be safe with her."

"Oh, you did? So then, what was your plan? Take Costa's money and run?"

"No, of course not. I would never run from my beautiful city. This is my home."

It was Ares who spoke up next. "Maybe you should just tell us what your plan was then."

"I thought it would have been obvious to someone like you, Ares. With Costa's money, I could pay the gangs and get them on our side. The alliance with them would be my gift to The Dark Kings, my payment for a seat at your table."

I had always known my cousin was an idiot, but even I had a hard time believing that his whole plan was to work with the Corsetti Family. Maybe this was his first step, but it definitely wasn't his last.

"What else?" I asked.

"Nothing else, I swear, Valentina. I just knew once they had you, I'd never see you again unless I had something to offer them."

"So your idea was to sell me for the money to see me? Mario, you sound like a fucking crazy person."

"Language, Valentina. Your father would never allow you to speak like that."

I pushed my chair back and stood, leaning over the table pointing in his direction. "My father is dead, you stupid fuck. If you gave a shit about anyone other than yourself, then maybe you could have done it yourself. That man deserved to die and you know it. Don't act like he was some great man who did great things, when the greatest thing he ever did was promise me to Dante. And he couldn't even do that right because he broke his fucking promise."

I felt Nico's hand on my back. I knew it was him. It didn't matter which one touched me. I always knew who it was because each of them felt so different to me. Mario went to stand but was forced back into his seat by one of the guards. Anton was sitting next to Ares and had his hand at the gun on his waist. Everyone was a little too trigger-happy tonight for my liking.

"Valentina, please, you can't possibly think everything your father did was wrong. He practically raised me. What kind of evil person takes in another person's child?"

"One who's own child was locked away in a cell for most of her life."

Mario shook his head as Dante stood up next to me. "I think we are done here. We will be in touch, Mario, but for now I wouldn't make any sudden moves." I reached for Dante's hand, and we all walked out of the room. Anton was close behind and whispering something into Ares' ear as we got to the elevator.

"I don't know if I want to stay out any longer," I said, turning to Dante.

"It's okay, my love, Ares will take you home with Anton. Nico will follow. I have a few things to take care of and then I will get on the road."

"Are you sure?"

"Absolutely," he leaned down and kissed me before turning to Anton, "I'll have them hold him until you are over the bridge."

Anton nodded and then we all got into the elevator. Dante rode down with us and said goodbye before heading back up to meet with Gina. I was suddenly cold and tired, and I wanted nothing more than to crawl into Dante's bed with Nico and Ares and wait for him. Ares took his coat off and draped it over my shoulders as we approached the SUV. I got in the back with him and Anton got behind the wheel. Nico got into his car and we pulled out of the garage.

"I thought Nico had somewhere to be tonight?"

"Not anymore. We are all going home."

I laid my head down onto Ares' lap as Anton drove. My calm peacemaker had more road rage than anyone I knew, but with Anton driving, I could close my eyes and hoped this whole mess would be over soon.

The phone ringing startled me before I could even doze off.

"Where?"

"And is he—"

"Fine. Pull over."

I sat up. Ares' entire demeanor had changed in the course in less than ten seconds.

The panic set in faster than I had hoped for. "What's wrong?"

"Pull over," he said, looking up into the rearview mirror at Anton, then he turned back to me, "I need to go with Nico. Anton's going to take you to the Penthouse. Stay there."

He leaned in to kiss me, but I held him back. "What happened?"

"Stay with Anton, Valentina. I'm serious. Don't go anywhere. We'll come back for you." He pushed forward and placed a kiss on my forehead, then opened the door and slammed it behind him. I looked out the back window as Anton sped off and watched Ares run to Nico's car and get in. They turned around and drove off in the opposite direction. Something truly awful must have happened for them to leave me. I was alone, and they all promised I wouldn't be alone again.

I pulled Ares' jacket around me, trying to keep the chill from my bones, but it wasn't cold. It was fear. I reached for my cell phone and called Dante's number. It rang and rang, but he didn't pick up. I dialed it again. Then again. I tried Ares and Nico, but they both sent me to voicemail.

"Valentina, you are safe with me. I won't let anything happen to you."

"What's going on? Where did they go?"

"I couldn't tell you even if I knew."

His words were cold, emotionless, and they only made things worse. I sat and stared out the window in silence until we pulled into the private garage of the penthouse. I didn't want to be here. I wanted to be home. Dante said we were going home, so it made no sense why Ares had Anton bring me here. The penthouse wasn't home; the Villa was.

I didn't move until Anton came around to open my door. Leo and Noah were already here, which was probably a bad thing. Not like they would tell me, anyway. I heard Anton on the phone talking to someone, but it just sounded like a muffled noise. Do you know that feeling when you're about to pass out? The one where everything looks kind of blurry and you have a loud ringing in your ears? That's what it feels like when your world is on the verge of falling apart.

Leo unlocked the door to the penthouse, which should have surprised me, but it didn't. I shuffled my way in, pulling Ares' jacket tight around my body as I walked to Dante's room, ignoring the crowd of men inside the apartment. Some of the guys looked up when I walked by, but most avoided looking at me all together. I didn't even bother to change my clothes. Instead, I just crawled into a ball on top of the covers and waited for someone to tell me what new hell I would be living in now.

Anton knocked on the door. I didn't bother looking up, but he came in anyway. "Valentina, I need to tell you something."

The tone of his voice gave him away, and the tears had started before I even knew what I was crying for. He stepped into my line of sight and said the three worst words I had ever heard.

"Dante's been shot."

WRATH: A DARK REVENGE MAFIA ROMANCE

Family wasn't blood, it was who you chose...

People feared my men, but that was only because they hadn't seen what I, Valentina Romano, was capable of. Torn apart by unfulfilled promises, hatred, and betrayal, I was done being a puppet in the games these men played.

I once considered him family, a close friend when I had no one else. Now he dared to ruin everything I had, everything we built, and for that he would die.

Ares Sabino, one of my three, always held me together. Now he'd be the one who helped me get my revenge. No one endangers my family and the world we created without paying for it. These challenges we faced were endless, but this was going too far.

Every day I wondered how much more we could take. Now I worried if this war I had declared would be what tore us all apart.

Get it Here: AMAZON

BEFORE YOU GO...

Please consider leaving a review on **Amazon**As an Indie author reviews are not only important to my business, but they are the biggest compliment. Even one word or a short line makes a world of a difference.

Books by Nikki Rome

Kindle Vella: Erotic Behavior: Sold to the Highest Bidder

The Corsetti Empire

Luca

Micah

Sofia

The Dark Kings

Greed – Novella

Lust

Envy

Wrath

The Heroes of Calvano Security

Unsettled Mind - Novella

Unbelievable

Unstoppable

Unbreakable

Unreasonable

Unexpected

Unrestrained

Saint Family Christmas

Jack's Second Chance

Nick's Secret Baby

Kane's Fake Relationship

Noelle's Secret Admirer

Eve's Marriage Pact

Holly's Injured Solider

About the Author

Nikki Rome has been a romance junky since a young age. As a girl she reached for book after book, looking for that happily ever after she always believed in. She loves all forms of romance and you can find her latest read not far from her reach. Nikki writes contemporary romance with a touch of danger. Her love of realistic characters who face real problems provides a story that touches the hearts of many. As a writer, reader and lover of words, it only made sense that she publish her stories. Her first series, The Heroes of Calvano Security, were first written for only her to enjoy. But now, years later, they are here for you along with so much more!

Newsletter Sign Up

Nikki's Naughty Romance Readers Group

www.NikkiRome.com
Info@NikkiRome.com

Instagram

Facebook

TikTok